OCEAN CITY WAVES

CLAUDIA VANCE

CHAPTER ONE

Outside Chipper's restaurant windows, Ocean City was settling into May, the streets not yet packed with the summer crowds that would arrive in just a few weeks. Inside, Lauren tallied the morning's receipts at the register while a few customers lingered over their cinnamon rolls and morning papers, the quiet hum of conversation replacing the earlier breakfast rush.

"Whoever's been using my good spatula as a doorstop better confess now!" Bobby called from the kitchen, his voice carrying over the clatter of pans being stacked.

Lauren overheard and chuckled as she picked up a coffee pot and walked to table six, topping off cups for an older couple who thanked her with quick nods. She'd been back to running Chipper's full-time for two months now, ever since she and Matt had finished their stint as off-season innkeepers at Starfish Cove Inn. The transition back had been smoother than she'd expected, like slipping into a favorite pair of jeans after wearing dress clothes for too long.

By twelve forty-five, the last customers had paid their checks and headed out. Lauren helped the servers wipe down tables while George and Bobby cleaned the kitchen. Chipper's only served breakfast, closing at one now instead of the old two-thirty closing time—a change Lauren had made to give the staff more reasonable hours. It meant her afternoons were completely free, a rhythm she'd grown to appreciate.

She stepped out the back door of Chipper's, the salt air immediately filling her lungs. The morning had warmed up nicely, and she could hear seagulls squabbling nearby. She was about to head to her car, then stopped. Maybe it was time for another look at the old store.

Her grandparents' shop, connected to Chipper's through the storage area, had sat untouched since the '90s. She'd shown it to Claire and Veronica last year, but she hadn't been back inside since. Now, with time on her hands, curiosity pulled her back toward the store.

Lauren retraced her steps through the kitchen, where Bobby barely glanced up from scrubbing the grill, and made her way through the storage area. The door to the store stood before her, unchanged. The front entrance on the street had been boarded up decades ago, but this back door from the restaurant still worked. She dug the keys from her purse and unlocked it, the click echoing in the quiet space.

The scent hit her first—mustiness mixed with old paper and something faintly floral, like potpourri that had lost its potency years before. She flipped on the light switch, and the fluorescent bulbs flickered to life overhead. One immediately popped and went dark, but the remaining lights cast a yellowish glow over everything.

Lauren stepped inside slowly, her footsteps leaving prints in the thin layer of dust coating the floor. It was just as she'd left it last year, yet somehow seeing it again still felt surreal—decades of memories layered over every shelf. The inventory remained untouched, as if her grandparents had planned to reopen the next day and that day simply never came.

She walked down the main aisle, trailing her fingers along the shelving units. The ribbon section still boasted hundreds of options—grosgrain next to satin, plaids beside florals, everything from quarter-inch widths to massive bows assembled and waiting. Dust motes swirled in the light streaming through cracks in the blacked-out windows. She remembered Beverly, the woman who used to make elaborate bows here, her skilled hands working wire and ribbon into works of art.

Moving deeper into the store, Lauren found the party supply section that had been her favorite as a child. Care Bears plates sat beside He-Man napkins. She spotted Smurfs table-cloths, Mickey Mouse centerpieces, and packages of themed invitations for birthdays long past. A box caught her eye—Cabbage Patch Kids party favors, still sealed in plastic. She picked up a pack of napkins featuring characters she barely remembered from Saturday morning cartoons. The price tag read a dollar twenty-nine.

Against the far wall, the craft section waited with its wreaths, garlands, and swags, alongside bins filled with decorative items. Faded silk flowers sat next to artificial fruit that had seen better days, miniature wooden animals beside strings of beads in every imaginable color. And because this was Ocean City, nautical touches were everywhere—brass anchors, miniature lighthouse figurines, tiny sailboats, and shell-shaped ornaments. She noticed a whole section dedicated to seasonal items too—Easter baskets, Fourth of July bunting, Halloween decorations with price tags from 1989.

Lauren turned a corner and stopped. A shelf of vintage toys lined the wall—Pound Puppies still in their original packaging, their felt faces peering through the plastic. She thought of Claire's Bowser, lost to a college move-out purge. So many childhood treasures, gone.

The store felt different today. Maybe it was the soft May light filtering through the cracks, or the solitude allowing her mind to wander. But standing here among the remnants of her grandparents' business, Lauren found herself transported not just to another decade, but to a different version of Ocean City entirely.

She wandered into a section she hadn't noticed before and discovered shelves of vintage beach toys. Plastic sand pails in faded primary colors, shovels with wooden handles, inflatable beach balls still in their packaging. A bin of shells, carefully sorted by type, each with a handwritten price tag in her grandmother's distinctive script. Another shelf held sun hats and visors, the fabric stiff with age, alongside bottles of suntan lotion with SPF numbers that would make any dermatologist cringe today.

Her phone buzzed in her pocket. She took it out to see Claire's name on the screen.

"Hey, sis," Lauren answered, glancing at a display of sun-bleached postcards.

"Lauren! We made it!" Claire's voice was bright with excitement, slightly breathless.

"Made it where?" Lauren asked, drifting to a shelf of children's books, their covers curled with age.

"To Ocean City! We're here! The moving truck just pulled up to the house on Beach Road. I'm standing in what's going to be our sunroom, and I can hear the waves from here. Lauren, this is really happening!"

Lauren's heart leapt. "You're here? Like, actually here? I thought you weren't coming until next week!"

"The kids just finished school, the movers had an opening, and I figured why wait? I can work from anywhere anyway, so here we are!"

Lauren could hear the smile in her sister's voice, could picture her standing in that empty house with Evan and Bridget probably already claiming bedrooms. Claire had been so excited when they'd found the place, a beautiful historical home.

"Wait, you drove the moving truck yourself?" Lauren asked.

Claire laughed. "No, I'm not that brave. I hired movers. But I did drive my car with both kids, which was its own kind of adventure. Anyway, I know you're probably busy, but I wanted to let you know we made it safely."

"That's amazing! How does the house look?"

"It's even better than the photos. The light in here is incredible—it's complete chaos here, but it's good chaos, you know?"

Lauren felt her shoulders relax. "I'm so glad you're here. This is going to be wonderful having you so close."

They said their goodbyes, and Lauren slipped her phone back into her pocket. She took one last look around the store, at the decades of merchandise waiting patiently in the dim light. This place deserved better than sitting idle and forgotten. Maybe, she thought, it was time to figure out what to do with all of this.

* * *

The drive down Beach Road was a short one. Lauren passed houses showing signs of the approaching summer season— yards being tidied, porches getting fresh coats of paint, and here and there she spotted groups of young people lugging suitcases into shared rental houses.

Beach Road ran parallel to the ocean, lined with a mix of newer construction and the occasional historical survivor. Lauren had always loved this street for its proximity to the beach, though she knew Claire had chosen it specifically for the rare gem she'd found—one of the original cottages that had somehow escaped demolition.

She spotted the pale-yellow cottage at once, standing out among the modern duplexes that flanked it on either side. A moving truck sat in the driveway, its back doors open. Lauren pulled up behind it and got out, taking in the full view of her sister's new home.

It was stunning. Two and a half stories of classic beach cottage architecture, with detailed trim work along the eaves and a sunroom at the front with original multi-pane windows facing the dunes. The green shutters provided a perfect contrast to the yellow siding. Flower beds lined the walkway, though they looked like they needed some attention.

"Hey, Aunt Lauren," Evan called from the porch. He and Bridget came down the steps, Bridget already reaching for a box from the truck.

"Hey, guys! How does it feel to be official Ocean City residents?"

"Amazing!" Bridget said, adjusting her grip on the box. "My room has a window seat, and I can see the beach!"

"Mine has a built-in bookshelf," Evan added. "The whole wall is shelves!"

Lauren grabbed a lamp from the truck. "That's perfect for you. I remember all those books you brought when you visited last summer."

Her parents' car drove up behind hers, and Lauren's parents climbed out.

"Moving day!" Joe called, heading toward the moving truck. "You didn't think we'd miss this, did you?" He grabbed a heavy box and hoisted it up with a grunt.

Nancy rolled her eyes. "Joe, your back. Remember what the doctor said."

"I'm just grabbing the light stuff, Nancy. Relax."

Claire appeared in the doorway, hair pulled back, wearing jeans and an old T-shirt. She looked happy but tired. "Mom! Dad! You didn't have to come."

"Of course we did," Nancy said, giving Claire a quick hug before surveying the truck. "Where do you want us to start?"

They fell into a rhythm, carrying boxes and furniture into the house. Lauren found herself on the stairs with a box labeled "Kitchen—Fragile" when she passed Claire going the opposite direction.

"Where's Brian?" Lauren asked casually. "Still wrapping things up in Pennsylvania?"

Claire's step faltered slightly. "Yeah, something like that. Hey, can you help me with something in the kitchen real quick?"

Lauren set her box down in the kitchen where Claire directed, then followed her sister out onto the back patio. The yard was overgrown, but the brick patio itself was in good shape, overlooking what could be a beautiful garden with some work.

Claire leaned against the railing, her back to the house. "He's not coming."

Lauren waited, giving her sister space to continue.

"The job offer fell through," Claire said finally, her voice quiet. "About six weeks ago. Brian got a call saying they'd decided to go with an internal candidate instead."

"That's awful," Lauren said.

"Yeah, well." Claire crossed her arms. "We were already under contract on this house. We'd found it, fallen in love with it, put down earnest money—everything was moving forward. But when Brian lost the job..." She paused. "He didn't want to come anymore. Not without the job. He said it didn't make sense to uproot everything without a job lined up."

Lauren's mind raced, trying to process this. "So what does that mean?"

"It means I still wanted to move. I'd already committed to this house, to the idea of being near you and Mom and Dad, of giving the kids this life at the beach. So I bought him out of his portion," Claire said, her tone matter-of-fact. "He's staying in Pennsylvania. We're... we're separating."

The word hung in the air between them.

"Separating," Lauren repeated, feeling like the ground had shifted beneath her. "Claire, when did all this happen?"

"I know. I know I should have told you sooner. But every time I tried to say the words, I just... couldn't. I had to get through it first."

Lauren pressed a hand to her mouth. "I'm so sorry. I wish

you'd told me. You shouldn't have been dealing with this alone."

"I wasn't alone. I had the kids. And my therapist," Claire added with a weak laugh. "But yeah, it's been... it's been a lot."

"Do Mom and Dad know?"

"Not yet. I need to tell them, I just haven't figured out how. They love Brian." Claire looked away. "Can you not say anything? Just for a few days? Let me get settled, get the kids adjusted, and then I'll sit down with them."

Lauren hesitated. Keeping something this big from their parents felt wrong, but Claire looked so exhausted, so fragile. "Okay. But Claire, you need to tell them soon. Like, this week."

"I will. I promise."

They went back inside, rejoining the organized chaos of moving day. Lauren caught herself watching Claire more carefully now, noticing the way she kept moving, restless, the way she threw herself into the physical work as if she could exhaust herself out of thinking.

The kids seemed to be handling things in their own way. Bridget kept running to her room to rearrange things, pouring all her energy into making her new space perfect. Evan had found the best reading spots in the house and kept making announcements about each one, his usual way of coping— retreating into books and routines.

Joe carried in a heavy box and set it down with a grunt. "That's the last of the big stuff. Just odds and ends left in the truck."

"Thanks, Dad," Claire said, giving him a one-armed hug. "You guys didn't have to do all this."

"That's what family's for," Nancy said, though she was eyeing Claire with the particular expression mothers get when they know something's off but can't quite put their finger on it.

Lauren jumped in quickly. "Claire, why don't you show Mom and Dad the upstairs? They haven't seen the view from the master bedroom yet."

As Claire led their parents upstairs, Lauren collected the last few boxes from the truck. The afternoon sun was starting to sink lower, casting long shadows across the street.

Two hours later, with the truck finally empty and most of the boxes at least in the right rooms, their parents headed home. Nancy made Claire promise to come for dinner later in the week, and Joe reminded her that he was just a phone call away if she needed anything fixed.

Lauren lingered, helping Claire break down the empty boxes and stack them by the garage.

"This is insane," Claire said, looking at the pile of cardboard. "How did we accumulate so much stuff?"

"Years of marriage and two kids," Lauren said. Then, realizing what she'd said, "Sorry, I didn't mean—"

"It's okay." Claire cut through another box with more force than necessary. "We did have years of marriage. That's just... that's just how it is now."

They worked in silence for a few more minutes before Lauren spoke again. "Have you thought about how you're going to explain it to people? To the kids?"

"The kids know. I told them a few weeks ago, after we finalized everything. They're upset, but they're also kids—they can be sad about their dad and excited about the house at the same time." Claire tossed another flattened box onto the pile. "As for everyone else... I don't know. I guess I'll figure it out as I go."

Lauren wanted to press further, to ask a hundred questions about what had led to this, whether there was any chance of reconciliation, how Claire was really doing. But her sister's weariness was palpable, and the house still looked like a disaster zone despite their efforts.

"I should let you get settled," Lauren said. "Rain check on the house tour?"

"Definitely. Maybe tomorrow once things calm down a bit." Claire managed a real smile. "Thanks for being here today. For listening. For not judging."

"Of course," Lauren said. "I'm here whenever you need me. Day or night."

As Lauren drove away from the cottage, she glanced in her rearview mirror to see Claire standing on the porch, arms wrapped around herself, looking small despite the charming house behind her.

Lauren's phone buzzed at a red light. A text from Matt: "Store's busy today. Stop by if you get a chance?"

She changed direction, heading toward the boardwalk. She needed to see him, to process everything Claire had just told her, to feel grounded again.

The boardwalk was busy for a weekday. Families strolled past with ice cream cones, teenagers clustered around the arcade, and the smell of pizza and funnel cakes drifted on the ocean breeze.

Jungle Surf sat at the far end, its colorful sign visible from several blocks away. Through the windows, Lauren could see movement, customers browsing the racks of clothing and surf gear.

She stepped inside Jungle Surf to the sound of Jack Johnson playing overhead and the distinct smell of surf wax and new cotton.

Matt looked up from behind the register where he was ringing up a customer, his face lighting up when he saw her. He held up one finger—just a minute—and finished the transaction.

"Hey," he said, coming around the counter once the customer left. "I wasn't sure if you'd make it."

"Hey," Lauren said, and the tightness in her expression made him pause.

"Everything okay?"

Lauren glanced around. A few customers were browsing the far wall, examining wetsuits. "Can we talk? Just for a minute?"

Matt called to Jake, one of his employees, who was

restocking shelves in the back. "Can you watch the register for a few?"

They stepped out onto the boardwalk, finding a relatively quiet spot by the railing overlooking the beach.

"Claire and Brian are separating," Lauren said, getting right to it. "She moved here without him. The job fell through, and he didn't want to come anymore."

Matt's eyebrows shot up. "What? When did this happen?"

"Apparently six weeks ago, but she just told me today. She swore me to secrecy from Mom and Dad, at least for a few days." Lauren leaned against the railing. "We spent two hours moving her in with our parents right there, and I had to pretend everything was fine."

"That's huge," Matt said. "How is she doing?"

"Honestly? I don't know. She's holding it together, you know? Just powering through. But I saw her face when she told me, and..." Lauren shook her head. "She's not okay. She's trying to be okay, but she's not."

Matt moved closer, his shoulder touching hers. "And how are you doing?"

"I'm worried about her. And I'm kind of hurt she didn't tell me sooner. I mean, I get it, she needed time to process, but six weeks? We talk almost every day." Lauren sighed. "I know that's selfish."

"It's not selfish. You're her sister. You want to be there for her."

"Lauren?" a voice called from behind them.

They both turned to see a tall woman with long dark hair pulled back in a ponytail, wearing shorts and a tank top that showed off tanned, athletic arms. She was holding a Jungle Surf shopping bag and staring at Lauren with widening eyes.

"Oh my gosh, Lauren Romano?"

Lauren squinted, trying to place the face. Something familiar about those eyes, that smile—

"Brenna? Brenna Groff?"

"Yes!" Brenna laughed, her smile widening. "I can't believe it's you! What are you doing here?"

"I live here now! Well, I moved here last year. And you? Last I heard you were in California, doing research."

"I was, but I got a position at the marine research center here. Started in March. I'm working on coastal ecology projects." Brenna's enthusiasm was infectious. "This is so crazy. I was just thinking about you the other day, wondering what you were up to."

"This is Matt," Lauren said, gesturing to him. "Matt, this is Brenna. We went to college together."

"Roommates sophomore year," Brenna added, shaking Matt's hand. "We had the smallest dorm room on campus but somehow made it work."

"Barely," Lauren said with a laugh. "Remember when we tried to fit that futon in there?"

"And your mini fridge," Brenna said. "I still don't know how we managed." She shifted her shopping bag. "Are you still in events? You were always so good at organizing things."

"Actually, I took over my family's restaurant. Chipper's. Do you know it?"

"The breakfast place with the amazing cinnamon rolls? I've been meaning to check it out. That's yours?"

"Family business, but yeah, I'm running it now."

"That's incredible." Brenna drew out her phone. "We should get together. Catch up properly. I'd love to hear what you've been up to all these years."

They exchanged numbers, making tentative plans to catch up soon. As Brenna walked away, calling out one more good-bye, Lauren turned back to Matt with a slight smile.

"Well, that was unexpected."

"Old friend?" Matt asked.

"Really old friend. We lost touch after college. I think the last time I saw her was at someone's wedding, maybe eight years ago?" Lauren watched Brenna disappear into the crowd.

"She was getting her master's in marine biology. Looks like that worked out."

"A coastal ecologist in Ocean City. That's a cool job."

"I bet."

Lauren's phone buzzed. A text from Claire: "Kids want to know if you can come to dinner tomorrow. I'm making lasagna. Mom and Dad coming too."

Lauren showed Matt the text. "Family dinner at Claire's new house. Where she'll presumably tell our parents about the separation."

"That'll be interesting."

"That's one word for it." Lauren typed back a quick yes. "I should let you get back to work. The place looks packed."

"It's been nonstop since about two," Matt admitted. "But I'm glad you stopped by."

They walked back into Jungle Surf together. Lauren watched him move through his shop with natural ease, greeting customers, answering questions about board sizes and wetsuit brands. This was his element, just as Chipper's was hers. As he helped a customer find the right board, her thoughts drifted to Claire, to Brian's absence, to Brenna's surprise reappearance. Everything felt like it was rearranging itself into new patterns.

CHAPTER TWO

The lift jerked upward with a metallic groan, and Maddie gripped the safety rail, her stomach lurching as the platform rose another five feet. She'd borrowed the lift from a contractor friend who'd warned her it was "temperamental," which apparently meant it made sounds like it might collapse at any moment.

"You good up there?" called a voice from below.

Maddie looked down to see Tyler, a college kid who worked at the french fry stand two shops down. He'd been watching her progress all morning.

"Define good," Maddie shouted back, steadying herself as the platform swayed slightly in the ocean breeze.

Tyler laughed. "Fair enough. You look like you could use a break."

"Maybe later!" Maddie called down, already refocusing on her work.

She was eighteen feet up the side of an arcade next to the former Gillian's Wonderland Pier, which had closed last year, armed with a paint roller, several gallons of acrylic, and a vision that had kept her up half the night sketching.

The arcade's owner had approached her five weeks ago

with an offer she couldn't refuse—paint whatever she wanted on the massive blank side wall visible from the boardwalk, as long as it was coastal-inspired, all materials provided. He was tired of looking at the chipped, faded white wall and wanted to beautify the area, he'd said, and the city had already approved the project. It was the kind of exposure artists dreamed about. Every tourist who walked to the pier would see it. Every local who grabbed pizza or fries would pass it multiple times a day.

Maddie wiped the sweat from her forehead with the back of her wrist, careful not to get paint in her eyes. Mid-May in Ocean City could be deceptively hot, especially when you were working in direct sunlight eighteen feet off the ground. Her tank top was already soaked through, and she'd only been at it for two hours.

She dipped her roller into the tray of cerulean blue and swept it across another section of sky. The mural was going to be massive—a stylized ocean scene featuring a wave curling over the boardwalk itself, as if the sea was reclaiming the land. Abstract enough to be interesting, realistic enough that people would recognize what they were looking at.

Below her, the boardwalk pulsed with its usual rhythm. Music drifted over from Playland's Castaway Cove, mixing with the screams from the rides and the splash of the water-park nearby. A group of teenagers walked past arguing about which pizza place had the best slice—Manco & Manco or Prep's. Two women pushed strollers, stopping to point up at Maddie's work-in-progress.

"That's going to be beautiful," one of them called up.

Maddie gave them a paint-splattered thumbs-up, turning her attention back to the section she was working on. The ocean portion would be the most challenging—she needed to capture that moment when a wave was suspended, translucent and powerful, right before it crashed. She'd spent years perfecting that effect in her smaller watercolors. Doing it on this scale, sixty feet long by twenty feet high, was going to be either her masterpiece or a very public failure.

The lift jerked again, and Maddie's heart skipped. She set down the roller and took a breath, gazing out over the ocean. From up here, she could see the full sweep of the beach, the water stretching to the horizon in shades of blue and green. Sailboats dotted the distance. Closer in, waves rolled toward shore in perfect sets.

Her phone buzzed in her pocket. She pulled it out to see a text from Regina, her employee who helped run her gallery, Coastal Wonders: "Gallery's slow today. Couple looking at the beach grass series. They said they'll be back tomorrow."

Maddie glanced at her watch. It was barely noon. She had hours of work ahead before she could even think about heading back. She typed a quick response: "Sounds good. Thanks for holding down the fort."

She tucked the phone away and picked up a smaller brush, switching to a darker blue to start adding depth to the water. This was the part that required precision—layering colors to create the illusion of movement.

A family stopped below, the father hoisting a small boy onto his shoulders so he could see better.

"Is she painting the ocean?" the boy asked.

"Looks like it," the father replied.

"But the ocean's right there." The boy pointed toward the beach, confused.

The mother laughed. "It's art, sweetie. She's making something pretty for everyone to enjoy."

The boy's question stuck with Maddie. Why paint the ocean when it was right there? Because anyone could photograph it. Her job was to convey something more—the power of it, the movement, the way it made you feel small and infinite at the same time.

She painted steadily for another hour, her shoulders aching from the repetitive motion of the brush. The sun beat down relentlessly. Her hair, tied back in a ponytail, kept escaping and sticking to her sweaty neck. She'd reapplied sunblock twice, and the wide-brimmed straw hat she'd bought specifically for this project was doing little to keep the heat at bay.

The music from the nearby miniature golf course changed to a new song, something upbeat and nostalgic. A seagull landed on the edge of the lift platform, eyeing her lunch bag with obvious interest.

"Not a chance," Maddie told it. "I've been up here too long to share my sandwich with you."

The bird squawked indignantly but stayed put, observing her progress with what looked like professional curiosity.

By one o'clock, Maddie's arms felt like lead, and the sun had shifted enough that she was working in her own shadow, which meant she needed to move the lift. She carefully climbed down, her legs shaky from being in the same position for so long.

"How's it looking?" Tyler asked, walking over from the fry stand with a water bottle.

"Like a half-finished mural," Maddie said, reaching for the bottle. "Thanks." She drained half of it in one go, then stepped back to assess her work from ground level. The sky was nearly complete, transitioning from light blue at the horizon to a deeper shade overhead. The wave was starting to take shape, though it still needed layers of detail.

"I can see where you're going with it," Tyler said, tilting his head. "It's going to be incredible when it's done."

"Thanks," Maddie said. "That's the hope, anyway. I should probably get back up there and—" She stopped mid-sentence. She'd spotted someone walking toward them down the board-walk, his stride confident, unmistakable even from a distance. Dominic.

He carried a large paper bag in one hand and two drinks in the other, navigating through the crowd with practiced ease. When he got closer, she could see he was wearing his usual work uniform—dark jeans and a fitted black T-shirt with "Dominic's Pizza & Subs" printed across the chest.

"Delivery for the artist," he announced, holding up the bag.

Maddie smiled. "What are you doing here?"

"Bringing you lunch," Dominic said, like it was the most obvious thing in the world. He set the bag down on a nearby bench and handed her one of the drinks. "Iced tea. Figured you'd need it working out here in this heat."

"I should probably get back to the stand," Tyler said, glancing between them with barely concealed amusement.

"Thanks, Tyler," Maddie said.

Tyler headed back toward the fry stand, leaving Maddie alone with Dominic.

"You didn't have to do this," Maddie said, though she was already opening the bag. The smell of fresh bread and marinara sauce made her stomach growl audibly.

"I know," Dominic said, settling onto the bench and pulling out his own sandwich. "But I was making lunch anyway, and I figured you probably forgot to eat. Artists always forget to eat."

"That's a stereotype," Maddie protested, though it was weakened by the fact that she had, in fact, forgotten to eat. She unwrapped the sandwich—a chicken parmesan sub that smelled amazing.

"How's the mural coming?" Dominic asked, glancing up at the wall.

"Slowly." Maddie took a bite of the sandwich and nearly groaned. It was perfect—the chicken was tender, the sauce rich, the bread had that ideal ratio of crispy outside to soft inside. "This is really good."

"Of course it is," Dominic said with that familiar confidence that had once annoyed her but now just made her smile. "My marinara sauce is legendary."

They ate in companionable silence for a few minutes, watching the flow of boardwalk traffic. A group of girls in bikinis and coverups walked past, ice cream cones in hand. A father chased after a toddler who'd decided to make a break for the beach.

"You're sweating like crazy up there," Dominic observed.

"It's hot," Maddie said with a shrug.

"Why didn't you start earlier in the morning? Before it got this bad?"

"Because I'm not a morning person," Maddie admitted. "I tried to set my alarm for six, but I kept hitting snooze."

Dominic laughed, and Maddie felt some of the exhaustion lift. It still surprised her sometimes, how easy this had become. Hard to believe they'd started out as bickering business neighbors.

"What about you? How's the restaurant?"

"Busy," Dominic said. "Getting busier every day."

"That's good."

"Yeah." He took a sip of his drink. "Though it means I've been at it nonstop. Hence the greasy hair and general disheveled appearance."

Maddie glanced at him. His hair did appear a bit more tousled than usual, and there was a smudge of what looked like flour on his forearm. But he didn't look disheveled so much as... lived-in. Like someone who'd been working hard at something he cared about.

"You should see me after eight hours of painting," she said. "I'm basically a Jackson Pollock piece."

"Now that I'd like to see," Dominic said, and there was something in his tone that made Maddie's cheeks flush in a way that had nothing to do with the heat.

She finished her sandwich and crumpled up the wrapper, their shoulders touching.

"I should get back to work," she said, standing up quickly. "The mural's not going to paint itself."

"Right." Dominic stood too, gathering up the trash. "You need anything else? More water? Snacks for later?"

"I'm good," Maddie said. She leaned in and kissed him quickly. "But thanks. For the lunch. It was thoughtful."

"Anytime," Dominic said, that half-smile playing at his lips.

He started to walk away then turned back. "Hey, Maddie?"

"Yeah?"

"The mural's really coming together. You've got an eye for this stuff."

Maddie smiled. "Thanks. That means a lot."

She watched him disappear into the boardwalk crowd, heading back to the pizza shop. Then she grabbed her water bottle and climbed back up the lift.

The afternoon stretched ahead, full of paint and possibility. As she picked up her brush and returned to the wave—adding highlights to suggest spray, shadows to create depth—Maddie found herself thinking about Dominic's words. About the way he'd shown up with lunch without being asked. About how natural it felt now, having someone in her corner.

She'd been dating him since Christmas—five months now. They'd taken it slow at first, both cautious after their rough beginning, but somewhere along the way it had become real. Dinners that turned into long conversations. Coffee on slow mornings that stretched into afternoons. Stolen moments between running their businesses.

But moments like this—him bringing her food and encouraging her work—made her wonder if maybe they were building toward something more substantial than either of them had planned.

The wave was taking shape now, layer by layer, that glassy, light-filled quality starting to emerge as she worked. She could almost see it moving, almost hear the crash it was about to make.

Below, the boardwalk continued its eternal rhythm. The rattle of skee-ball, voices calling out, the smell of pizza and popcorn and ocean salt. This was Ocean City in May, balanced on the edge of summer, full of potential and promise.

Maddie dipped her brush in white paint and added some highlights to the crest of the wave, watching as it came alive under her hand.

* * *

Lauren stood on the front walk of Claire's new house, seeing it properly for the first time. The day before had been all chaos—boxes and furniture and endless trips to and from the truck. She'd barely registered the house itself beyond room layouts and which door led where.

Now, in the quiet afternoon light, she could actually look at it.

The pale-yellow siding glowed warm in the sun, and the green shutters framed windows with wavy glass—the real thing, not reproduction. The brick path she'd walked a dozen times during the move was lined with overgrown boxwoods that needed trimming but somehow added to the cottage's charm. From here, Lauren could hear the distant rush of waves—the house sat just across the street from the dunes.

"Now you can see the place without tripping over boxes," Claire said, opening the front door.

"It's wonderful," Lauren said honestly. "Claire, this house is stunning."

"Come on, let me give you the real tour. You were too busy helping me move boxes to take it all in."

They stepped into the sunroom, and Lauren stopped. The day before, this room had been full of boxes labeled "FRAG-ILE" and furniture wrapped in blankets. Now she could take it in—flooded with natural light from windows on three sides, each offering a different view. To the right, across the street, the dunes rose up, blocking the ocean from direct view but allowing the rush of waves to drift through. Straight ahead, neighboring yards with wild rose bushes.

"This is the only room I've managed to unpack properly."

Claire gestured to a cream-colored couch positioned to face the beach, with a coffee table and two armchairs completing the seating area. "Bridget was out here this morning reading."

The sunroom floors were pine, worn smooth by a century of footsteps, and the ceiling featured exposed beams that Lauren hadn't noticed on moving day. Plants sat on the windowsills—succulents and a few struggling spider plants that Claire had transported from Pennsylvania.

"The first owners used this as a breakfast room," Claire explained. "They'd eat meals here to catch the sunrise. The real estate agent showed me old photos—there was this built-in bench seating along the windows."

"Come see the living room." Claire motioned, leading the way through a wide doorway.

If the sunroom was bright and airy, the living room was cozy and grounded. The ceiling was lower here, with original beams that had been painted white decades ago. A brick fireplace dominated one wall, its mantel thick with layers of old paint. Built-in bookshelves flanked the fireplace, and Claire had already started filling them.

"Those shelves came with the house." She ran her hand along the wood. "According to my agent, they were added in the 1920s when the cottage was expanded. Everything else dates to 1890."

"1890," Lauren breathed, trying to imagine the house as it had been then. "So it's been through everything—the 1927 fire that destroyed the boardwalk, the Great Hurricane of 1944, the Depression, two world wars, the Ash Wednesday Storm."

"I know," Claire said quietly. "That's part of what I love about it. This house has weathered so much, and it's still standing."

The living room furniture was an eclectic collection—the couch from their Pennsylvania house appeared too modern for the space, and the flat-screen TV mounted above the fireplace felt jarring against the antique architecture. But there were touches that worked perfectly: a vintage trunk Claire used as a coffee table, an old brass lamp, handmade crochet pillows in natural linen and sage.

"Kitchen's through here." Claire gestured toward the doorway.

The kitchen had clearly been updated in the past decade, though whoever had done it had tried to maintain the cottage feeling. White cabinets with glass fronts showed off mismatched dishes. The counters were butcher block, practical. A farmhouse sink sat under a window that opened onto the backyard.

"I'm going to replace the appliances eventually," Claire said, opening the refrigerator to reveal a pack of water bottles and not much else. "But that's low priority compared to the bathroom situation."

"What's wrong with the bathroom?"

"Come see."

They climbed the stairs—creaking with each step—and Claire led her down a hallway with sloped ceilings and uneven floors.

"This is the kids' bathroom." Claire pushed open a door.

The bathroom was tiny, with a pedestal sink, a toilet, and a claw-foot tub that barely fit in the space. But it was also perfect—black-and-white tile floor in a basket weave pattern, period fixtures, a window with frosted glass that let in soft light.

"It's charming," Lauren said.

"It's also constantly running," Claire said. "The toilet, I mean. And the tub faucet drips no matter how tight you turn it. I have a plumber coming next week."

The kids' bedrooms were small but warm, each with sloped ceilings and dormer windows. Bridget had already personalized hers with posters and a few favorite stuffed animals. Evan's was still mostly boxes, though he'd set up his desk under the window.

"And this is the master." Claire pushed open the door at the end of the hall.

The room was larger than Lauren expected, spanning the width of the house. Windows on two walls let in cross breezes, and there was another small fireplace in the corner—decorative now, but Claire said it had been functional once.

"The closet is ridiculous," Claire said, opening a door to reveal a space barely big enough for hanging clothes. "But I don't care. Look at this view."

She walked to the open window, and Lauren joined her. From this height, the dunes no longer blocked the view—the beach and ocean stretched out before them.

"I was here this morning with my coffee, just watching," Claire said.

They lingered in silence, the sound of waves a constant backdrop.

"How are you doing?" Lauren asked, watching her sister's profile.

Claire crossed her arms, still looking out the window. "I don't know. Some moments I'm fine. I'm excited about the house, about the kids being close to you and Mom and Dad. Other moments I'm terrified. What if I made the wrong choice? What if I should have fought harder to make it work with Brian?"

"Do you think you should have?"

Claire didn't answer right away. She stared out the window. "No," she said finally. "We weren't happy, Lauren. We hadn't been for a while. The job falling through was just the catalyst. But knowing it was the right decision doesn't make it easier."

"Have you heard from him?"

"A few times. Mostly about logistics—when he wants to FaceTime with the kids, questions about bills that were in my name." Claire rubbed her temples. "It's so weird, going from talking every day to these formal exchanges about practical stuff."

"I'm sorry."

"Don't be." Claire turned away from the window. "I made this choice. I chose this house, this life, being near family. I'm not sorry about that. I'm just... adjusting."

They went back downstairs, and Claire led her to the back porch—a screened-in space that overlooked the jungle of a backyard.

"This needs work too," Claire said, gesturing to the wild garden beds and patches of tall grass. "But I keep thinking about what it could be. A vegetable garden, maybe. Some fruit trees. A space where the kids can play."

"It has potential," Lauren agreed, eyeing what appeared to be an old shed in the far corner.

"So," Claire said, settling into a weathered wicker chair. "Mom and Dad are coming for dinner tonight. Which means I need to tell them about Brian."

"Are you ready?"

"No." Claire laughed, but it sounded strained. "But I can't avoid it forever. They're going to notice that Brian never shows up. And the kids might say something."

"Do you want me to be there?"

"Would you?" Claire looked relieved. "I know it's family drama, but having you there might make it easier."

"Of course I'll be there."

They spent the next hour getting the living room in order, filling bookshelves and shifting furniture until things felt right. The work was comfortable and quiet, both of them lost in their own thoughts.

Around five, Lauren helped Claire start dinner—lasagna, Claire's specialty, assembled and ready to go in the oven. They made a salad, set the table, and opened wine.

Joe and Nancy arrived at six, bearing a pie and cheerful commentary about the house.

"You've already made it feel like home," Nancy said,

walking through the sunroom with obvious appreciation. "Claire, you have such an eye for these things."

"Where's Brian?" Joe asked, glancing around as if he might have missed him. "Still wrapping things up back home?"

The room went quiet. Claire glanced at Lauren then took a breath.

"Actually, Dad, we need to talk about that." She gestured to the living room. "Can everyone sit down for a minute?"

The kids were out back, playing ladder ball, their voices drifting in through the screen porch.

They settled into chairs—Nancy and Joe on the couch, Lauren in an armchair. Claire remained standing.

"Brian's not coming," Claire said without preamble. "We're separating."

Nancy's hand went to her mouth. Joe sat forward, elbows on his knees.

"The job offer fell through about six weeks ago," Claire continued, her voice steady but quiet. "And when it did, Brian decided he didn't want to move without it. We tried to figure out if there was a way to make it work—him staying there, me here—but we both knew it wasn't sustainable. I bought him out of his portion of the house. He's staying in Pennsylvania."

"Oh, honey," Nancy said, stunned. "Why didn't you tell us?"

"Because I had to focus on the logistics," Claire said. "I needed to pack up our life, make the move, get the kids settled. I couldn't fall apart in the middle of all that."

Joe was silent, his expression unreadable. Lauren knew that look—he was processing, trying to figure out what to say, what to do.

"Do the kids know?" Nancy asked.

"They know. We told them together before I finalized everything. They're upset, but they're handling it." Claire's voice cracked slightly. "They're resilient."

"Are you okay?" Joe asked, his voice gruff. "Because you don't have to be. You're allowed to not be okay."

Claire's eyes welled up, but she took a breath and steadied herself. Nancy rose and put a hand on her arm.

"I'm okay," Claire said. "Really. It's just been a lot."

"What can we do?" Nancy asked.

"You're here. That's enough."

They called the kids in from the backyard and moved to the dining room for dinner. Claire's lasagna was perfect—layers of ricotta and meat sauce, the cheese on top golden and bubbling. They passed around the salad and warm garlic bread, the conversation gradually returning to normal topics— Joe's latest woodworking project, Nancy's book club, Bridget's upcoming soccer tryouts.

As the evening wound down and her parents prepared to leave, Lauren found herself standing in the sunroom again, looking out at the dunes. The sun was setting, painting the sky in shades of pink and orange. She could hear Claire laughing at something their father said, hear the kids upstairs getting ready for bed.

This house, with its creaking floors and antique windows, its history and its imperfections, felt like exactly where Claire needed to be.

At least, Lauren hoped so.

CHAPTER THREE

Nancy gripped the steering wheel tighter as Joe laughed from the passenger seat.

"I'm serious, Joe. I can't wait anymore."

"We're five minutes from home."

"I don't care. I'm stopping at the Welcome Center."

They'd just crossed from Somers Point onto the bridge, the bay spreading out on either side, boats dotting the water in the morning light. The Welcome Center sat on the right side of the bridge, a building with parking spaces and bathrooms that Nancy had driven past countless times without stopping. But today, after spending the morning running errands on the mainland, followed by breakfast where Nancy had consumed two full cups of coffee, her bladder was staging a rebellion.

"You're ridiculous," Joe said, still grinning as Nancy pulled into the parking lot.

"You're the one who kept telling the waitress to top me off."

"I was being helpful. You could have said no."

Nancy parked and practically jogged toward the bathroom entrance. "I'll be right back."

"Take your time," Joe called after her. "I'll be out here, not dying of bladder failure."

Inside, the bathroom was mercifully clean and empty. Nancy emerged five minutes later feeling considerably better, finding Joe standing at the railing that overlooked the bay and marshland beyond. But he wasn't alone. A small group of people had gathered, pointing toward the trees, their voices excited.

"What's going on?" Nancy asked, joining him.

Joe pointed toward the trees. "Birds. Lots of them."

Nancy followed his gesture, and her breath caught. There they were—dozens, maybe hundreds of white birds dotting the green marsh trees like snow in spring. "Wow. What are they?"

"In those trees right there," said a woman standing nearby, binoculars raised to her eyes. "White ibises, egrets, and herons. They're nesting."

"Nesting?" Nancy moved closer to the railing. "Right here by the bridge?"

"They nest from spring through early summer," the woman explained. "This colony's been here for years, but not everyone knows about it. People drive right past without looking." She lowered her binoculars and smiled. "Would you like a closer look? I have an extra pair."

She handed Nancy a pair of binoculars, and Nancy raised them to her eyes, fumbling with the focus wheel. For a moment she saw nothing but blurred green, then the image sharpened, and suddenly the world came into focus.

Through the binoculars, the scene came alive with detail. Great white egrets, their long, elegant necks extended, their plumage pristine. Smaller snowy egrets darted between branches. The ibises were easy to spot with their distinctive curved beaks. A great blue heron glided past, its wide wings catching the light. And mixed among them all, darker shapes that the woman identified as night herons.

"Amazing," Nancy breathed. "Joe, look at this."

She handed him the binoculars, and he raised them slowly. His mouth opened slightly as the focus adjusted. "Holy..."

"Right?" The woman laughed. "It's something, isn't it? I come here three times a week during nesting season. You can see eggs in some of the nests if you look carefully."

Nancy took the binoculars back, scanning the trees more slowly now. And there—in a nest near the top of a dead tree—she could just make out the pale shape of eggs, three of them, with an egret settled protectively on top.

"They're nesting right here," Nancy said wonderingly. "Right beside the bridge."

"Birds are adaptable," the woman said. "This marsh provides everything they need—fish, crabs, shelter. They don't care about the traffic."

A man joined them at the railing, his own binoculars around his neck. "First time seeing the rookery?"

"Rookery?" Joe asked.

"That's what they call a nesting colony of waterbirds," the man explained. He looked to be in his seventies, with tanned, weathered skin. "I've been coming here since they opened the Welcome Center. The egrets and herons have been here forever, but the white ibises—those are new. They only started nesting here in 2020. Now the whole rookery's exploded. They counted close to a thousand ibises last spring."

Nancy trained the binoculars on a different section of trees. An egret was landing on a branch, carrying a stick in its beak, adding it to the nest structure. Another egret stood nearby, watching, and Nancy could have sworn she saw them exchange a signal, a slight bob of their heads, before the first bird continued its work.

"Can I see again?" Joe asked, and Nancy reluctantly handed over the binoculars.

They took turns for the next twenty minutes, passing the binoculars back and forth, marveling at the activity in the trees. The woman with the extra binoculars introduced herself as Lori, and her husband was the weathered man, whose name was Eric. They were locals, retired, and bird-watching had become their shared passion.

"You see that white ibis there?" Eric pointed. "The one with the chick?"

Nancy looked through the binoculars, finding the nest he meant. A dark-colored chick sat in the nest, its beak open, while the adult ibis appeared to be feeding it. "Is that the baby?"

"Chick," Eric confirmed. "They're dark when they hatch and won't turn mostly white for a couple of years. That one's probably a few weeks old, still dependent on the parents for food."

"What do they eat?" Joe asked.

"Small fish, insects, crustaceans. They wade in the shallows, probing with those curved beaks. Very efficient hunters."

Nancy watched the ibis feed its young, mesmerized by the interaction. She and Joe had summered in Ocean City for decades before retiring here, had driven over this bridge many times, and she'd never known this was here. Never stopped to look. Never realized that just beneath the bridge, hidden in plain sight, was this whole world of birds living their lives, building nests, raising chicks, entirely unconcerned with the human activity around them.

"They migrate, right?" Joe asked, still watching through the binoculars.

"The ibises migrate south for the winter," Lori said. "They leave by October and come back in spring. The egrets and herons mostly migrate too, though during mild winters you might see a few that stay. You'll see different species depending on the season."

"And they come back to the same spot every year?" Nancy asked.

"They do. That's what makes rookeries so important—they're traditional nesting sites, used generation after generation. Destroying one doesn't just disrupt that year's breeding. It can break a pattern that's been established for decades."

Nancy thought about that—the ibises and egrets returning here year after year, trusting in the consistency of this place, building their lives around it. It seemed both fragile and remarkably resilient. The birds adapted to the highway noise, to the boats passing in the bay, to the human presence that surrounded them. They found a way to thrive despite everything.

"There," Eric said suddenly, pointing. "Watch that nest—the mate's coming in."

Nancy found it in the binoculars—a great egret gliding in from the bay. It landed beside another egret already on the nest, and she watched as the two birds stretched their necks toward each other, bills nearly touching. Then the arriving bird settled in while its mate spread its wings and took off, its wingspan stretching several feet as it headed out over the water.

"Beautiful," Nancy murmured.

"Most people don't stop to notice," Lori said. "They're in such a hurry, rushing home or to the beach. They miss all this."

Nancy lowered the binoculars, looking at Joe, who was watching the rookery with wonder on his face. In all their years of marriage, she'd seen that expression on his face maybe a handful of times—when each of their daughters was born, when they'd hiked to the top of a mountain in Colorado and seen the view, when he'd finished building a treehouse for the girls and stood back to admire it.

"We should come back," Nancy said quietly.

"With our own binoculars," Joe agreed.

Lori smiled. "You've caught the bug. That's what Eric said when I dragged him out here the first time. Now he's out here more than I am."

They stayed for nearly an hour, watching the constant activity. Birds flew in and out, bringing food to their nests, tending their eggs, building and repairing their homes.

As they finally walked back to the car, Nancy felt something shift inside her. She'd come to the Welcome Center out of desperation, needing a bathroom. She was leaving with something else entirely—a sense of discovery, of connection to this place they called home.

* * *

The newly renovated baseball field sat in the northern part of Ocean City, tucked away from the main beach blocks but still close enough to hear the ocean. Matt pulled into the gravel parking lot at seven thirty, the evening air still holding the day's heat. Jason and Tom were already there, leaning against Jason's pickup truck.

"About time," Jason called. "We were about to start without you."

Matt grabbed his glove from the passenger seat. He'd found it in his closet last week while looking for beach chairs, buried under old surfing magazines and unopened mail. The leather was stiff from years of disuse, and the pocket needed breaking in again, but holding it had transported him back instantly— familiar in a way that stirred something in his chest.

"Place looks incredible," Tom said as they walked toward the field. "Remember when this was just dirt and weeds?"

The transformation was remarkable. The outfield grass had been freshly cut and lined, the infield dirt raked smooth. New dugouts flanked home plate, and the bases gleamed white in the fading daylight. But it was the light towers that caught Matt's attention—four of them, standing tall at each corner of the field, their bulbs dark for now but promising.

"They're turning the lights on tonight for the first time," Jason said. "The parks and rec guy mentioned it when I ran into him at Wawa. Figured we'd come see it."

Matt stepped through the chain-link fence and onto the field proper. The smell of fresh dirt and cut grass hit him, and suddenly he was twenty-two again, walking out to the bullpen at Veterans Stadium in Philadelphia. His first call-up to the majors. He'd felt invincible then, his fastball hitting ninety-six on the radar gun consistently. He'd been so certain his career stretched ahead of him, years of pitching in meaningful games.

"You okay?" Tom asked.

Matt realized he'd stopped moving, standing at the edge of the infield with his glove hanging at his side. "Yeah. Just taking it in."

They tossed the ball around for a while, working out the kinks, their throws growing more confident as muscles remembered old patterns. Jason's arm had always been stronger than Matt's, even back in high school, but Jason had chosen surfing over baseball. Tom had played shortstop in college, and it showed in how cleanly he fielded grounders.

The sky deepened from blue to purple, and Matt was about to suggest they call it when headlights swept across the gravel. A van pulled up, and a group of men in matching gray jerseys climbed out, laughing and ribbing each other.

"Oh good, other people," Jason said. "I was starting to feel like we were trespassing."

One of the men—mid-forties, stocky, with a beard going gray at the edges—approached them. "You guys here for the beer league?"

"Beer league?" Matt asked.

"Yeah, Ocean City Adult Baseball League. We've got teams forming for the summer season. Tonight's just a practice to check out the new field." He extended his hand. "I'm Dan. I manage the Shorebreak."

They shook hands around, introducing themselves.

"We're short players," Dan continued. "Lost three guys this month—two moved, one's got a baby at home and his wife said no more weeknight games." He laughed. "You guys play?"

"Long time ago," Matt said carefully.

"High school," Jason added.

Dan's eyes lit up. "Even better. Look, we could use three more bodies if you're interested. Games are scattered throughout the summer, weeknight evenings. Nothing crazy competitive, just guys who like baseball and beer, in that order." He grinned. "What do you say?"

Matt glanced at Jason and Tom. Jason shrugged, already smiling. Tom nodded.

"Sure," Matt heard himself say. "Why not?"

"Excellent. Let me get you fitted with some jerseys. We've got extras in the van."

As Dan jogged back to the parking lot, his teammates started spreading out across the field, taking positions. One of them carried a bucket of baseballs toward the mound.

"Guess this is happening," Tom said.

Dan returned a minute later with jerseys and tossed one to each of them. "Wear these next time. Tonight, just have fun."

The lights clicked on then flooded the field with brightness. Matt's breath caught. The effect was instant and complete— shadows cut sharp across the dirt, the night sky vanishing beyond the glow. Suddenly it could have been any field, anywhere. It could have been the Phillies' stadium. It could have been a minor league stadium somewhere in Pennsylvania.

It could have been the night everything changed.

Matt was standing on the mound before he'd consciously decided to walk there. The rubber felt solid under his foot as he toed it, testing his position. His shoulder twinged—not painfully, just a reminder that it was there, that it had broken down once before.

"You pitch?" one of Dan's teammates called from behind home plate, squatting into a catcher's stance.

"Used to," Matt called back.

"Want to throw a few? I'm Braxton, by the way."

Matt lifted his arm and worked it in slow circles, feeling the surgery scar tissue stretch and pull, familiar but foreign. Two decades since he'd pitched competitively. Two decades since the doctor had told him his career was over, that the tear in his labrum was too severe, that even after surgery his velocity would never return.

But that had been in high-pressure professional baseball, where a drop from ninety-six to eighty-nine meant you were done. This was beer league. This was weeknights with guys who worked construction and ran surf shops and probably couldn't hit ninety on their best day.

Jason appeared beside him. "You sure about this?"

"No," Matt admitted. "But I want to try."

Jason picked up a ball from the bucket and flipped it to him. "Then let's see what you've got."

The leather felt right in his hand—the seams under his fingers, the weight of it, the way it nestled into his palm. Matt went through his old routine: deep breath, check the sign even though the catcher wasn't giving any, wind up. His body remembered the motion even as his mind questioned it. Leg kick, gather, drive toward the plate, let it go.

The ball sailed wide and high, bouncing off the backstop.

"Might need a few more," Braxton said, throwing it back.

Matt caught it and threw again. The tightness was there but not the sharp pain he'd feared. Another throw, this time finding the general vicinity of the strike zone. Then another. And another.

Most of his pitches were wild—some bouncing in the dirt, others sailing high. His mechanics felt foreign, his release point inconsistent. A few crossed the plate, but more by luck than design. The catcher had to work to track them down.

"You'll get there," Braxton called encouragingly after another ball that nearly hit him in the shin.

The burn started deep in the joint. Not the sharp tear of injury, but the dull fatigue of muscles pushed past their limits.

He threw a few more pitches, each one a little worse than the last, his arm losing steam with every throw.

Some of the guys were playing catch, others taking practice swings. It was loose, informal—exactly what Matt needed.

Matt threw for another few minutes before his body told him it was done. Most of his final throws barely made it to the plate. When he finally stepped off the mound, his arm hung at his side, spent.

"Hey, at least you got it over the plate a couple times," the catcher said, clapping him on the shoulder. "That's a start."

Matt nodded, testing the joint carefully. "I think I'm done for tonight. Don't want to push it too hard the first time out."

"Smart," Dan said, overhearing. "Last thing you need is to blow it out before the season even starts."

Jason glanced at Tom then at Matt. "We should probably head out too."

"Sounds good. See you guys at the next one," Dan said, while shaking their hands.

When Matt finally walked off the field with Jason and Tom, past nine, his arm felt like dead weight. The team continued their practice under the lights behind them. He'd thrown more pitches tonight than in the last twenty years combined. Tomorrow he'd pay for it—the stiffness would set in, the old injury reminding him of its presence. But right now, he felt something he hadn't felt in years.

He felt like a pitcher again.

"So we're doing this?" Jason asked as they reached the parking lot. "The beer league?"

"I'm in," Tom said immediately.

Matt stretched, feeling the soreness, the ache, but also the satisfaction. "Yeah," he said. "I'm in."

Dan caught up with them, handing over a schedule printed on crumpled paper. "Here's the lineup for the summer. Check the dates and let me know which ones you can make."

"Will do," Matt said. He glanced at the schedule, noting

games marked for various weeknights over the next few months, then folded it and tucked it into his pocket.

As Matt drove home, his shoulder throbbing but his mind clear, he replayed the night in his head. The ball leaving his hand. The mound beneath him. The glow of the field against the dark sky. He wondered if his arm would ever find its rhythm again, or if tonight was as good as it would get.

CHAPTER FOUR

The breakfast rush at Chipper's had tapered off twenty minutes ago. A few last customers sat scattered across the dining room, in no rush to finish. Lauren wiped down the counter near the register, mentally reviewing the supply order she'd need to place that afternoon. George was restocking the kitchen for tomorrow, and she could hear Bobby humming off-key as he scrubbed the grill.

The bell above Chipper's front door chimed, and Lauren looked up from the register to see Claire walking in with Bridget and Evan trailing behind her.

"Hey!" Lauren said, surprised. "I didn't know you were coming by."

"We needed to get out of the house," Claire said, sliding onto a stool at the counter. "I've been unpacking boxes for three days straight, and if I look at another piece of packing tape, I'm going to lose it." She glanced at the kids. "Plus, their school finished last week, so they've been bouncing off the walls with nothing to do."

Bridget claimed the stool next to her mother while Evan wandered toward the window, already pulling out his phone.

"What can I get you guys?" Lauren asked, grabbing three menus even though she knew they probably didn't need them.

"Pancakes," Bridget said immediately. "With chocolate chips."

"Scrambled eggs and toast," Claire said. "And coffee. Lots of coffee."

"Evan?" Lauren called.

He glanced up from his phone. "French toast?"

Lauren put their order in with George, who grunted acknowledgment, then poured Claire's coffee.

"How's the unpacking going?" Lauren asked, leaning against the counter.

"Slowly," Claire said, wrapping her hands around the coffee mug. "I found seventeen different boxes labeled 'miscellaneous,' which is apparently what I thought was a useful system at the time. Yesterday I unpacked a box that had kitchen utensils mixed with bathroom stuff and winter scarves. It made no sense."

"Did you at least find everything important?"

"Define important. I found the coffee maker, so that's what matters." Claire took a long sip. "But I'm still missing half my baking dishes and the box with all our board games."

George rang the bell, then Lauren brought over their food, setting plates in front of each of them. Evan dug into his French toast immediately while Bridget carefully arranged her pancakes before taking a bite.

"Actually," Lauren said, glancing toward the kitchen where George and Bobby were deep in conversation. "I've been thinking about the store next door."

Claire raised an eyebrow, interested. "Yeah?"

"Someone called last week wanting to buy everything," Lauren said. "Some vintage dealer from Pennsylvania. He offered a flat rate to clear out the whole place."

"Did you take it?"

"No. I didn't call him back." Lauren crossed her arms. "I

don't know. Part of me thinks I should just sell it all and be done with it. But another part feels like that's giving up on something."

"What would you do with it otherwise?"

"That's the question. I keep going back and forth. Open it again? Sell things online? Just let it sit there collecting more dust? It feels like it needs something, you know? Like it's been waiting all these years for someone to figure out what to do with it."

Claire set down her fork. "Can we go look at it? I haven't been back since you showed it to me last year."

"Seriously?"

"Why not? You're closing soon anyway, and I'm desperate for any activity that doesn't involve unpacking." Claire turned to her kids. "You guys want to see something cool? Your great-grandparents' old store?"

Bridget looked skeptical. "Like what?"

"Old store full of vintage stuff from the eighties," Claire said. "Think of it as a museum."

They finished eating while Lauren handled the last few customers, Bridget scrolling through Claire's phone and Evan staring out the window at the street.

By twelve forty-five, the last customer had left and George was finishing up in the kitchen. Lauren grabbed her keys and led Claire and the kids through the storage area to the connecting door.

The door creaked open, and that familiar scent of dust and old paper filled the air. Lauren flipped on the lights, the fluorescent bulbs casting their yellowish glow over everything.

"Whoa," Bridget said, stepping inside. "This is amazing."

They spread out, each drawn to different sections. Bridget immediately gravitated toward the party supplies, marveling at character plates and napkins she'd only seen in pictures online. Evan found the vintage toy section and stopped in front of the Pound Puppies display.

"Look at these price tags," Claire said, examining a package of Care Bears napkins. "Ninety-five cents. Can you imagine?"

Lauren moved toward the back of the store, an area she hadn't fully explored the last time she'd been here. Behind the main shelving units, she found a small office space—really just a desk and some filing cabinets crammed into a corner.

"Claire, come look at this."

Her sister joined her, peering around the shelf. "An office?"

"I didn't even notice this before." Lauren pulled open the top drawer of the nearest filing cabinet. It was full of old invoices, yellowed with age and organized by month and year. "These go back to 1980."

Claire opened another drawer. "Order forms. Vendor catalogs. Everything's handwritten."

"They were meticulous," Lauren said, running her fingers along a row of ledgers on the desk. She pulled one out—1986, the cover read in her grandmother's neat script. She opened it carefully, the spine cracking slightly.

A stack of photographs slipped out and scattered across the desk.

"Oh," Claire said softly, picking one up. "Lauren."

It was a photo of the store's interior, probably from the mid-eighties based on the visible inventory. The colors had faded slightly with age, but their grandmother was clear—standing behind the counter, smiling at the camera, wearing an apron with the store's name embroidered across it. A customer—a woman with two small children—was examining something on the shelves in the background.

Lauren picked up another photo. This one showed their grandfather outside the front entrance, which was still accessible from the street back then. The awning was bright and new, and a hand-painted sign announced a summer sale.

"I've never seen these," Claire said, flipping through more

photos. "Here's one of the ribbon section with that woman, what was her name? Beverly?"

"Beverly," Lauren confirmed, studying the image. The woman was mid-bow-making, her hands a blur of motion, ribbon cascading around her workstation.

There were more—customers browsing, employees restocking shelves, a photo of what looked like a busy Saturday with the store packed full of people. Their grandparents captured in their element, building something that mattered.

Claire pulled a folded piece of newspaper from between the ledger's pages. She unfolded it carefully—the paper was brittle and yellowed. "June 1985," she read.

It was a feature article about local businesses. A photograph showed their grandparents standing in front of the store, and the headline read: "Romano's Party & Gift Shop Celebrates Fifth Anniversary."

Lauren leaned over to read the article. It talked about how the store had become a community staple, how people came from neighboring towns for the selection of ribbons and party supplies, how the family-run business was thriving alongside Chipper's.

"1985," Claire said. "Over forty years ago. It's crazy seeing it all documented like this."

Lauren looked at the photos spread across the desk. "They put so much into this place."

They spent the next twenty minutes going through what they found—more photos tucked into different ledgers, a few more newspaper clippings, notes in the margins about special orders and regular customers. Nothing earth-shattering, but seeing their grandparents' life in the store documented this way felt significant.

Bridget appeared beside them. "What'd you find?"

"History," Lauren said, holding up a photo of their grandmother. "Your great-grandmother ran this place."

"So what are you going to do?" Claire asked, leaning against the desk.

Lauren looked around at the shelves, the inventory, the decades of accumulated merchandise. "I don't know. The practical thing would be to sell it all. I'm already running Chipper's full-time. Do I really need another project?"

"Maybe you don't need it," Claire said slowly. "But maybe you want it."

"What would I even do with a store like this?"

Claire pushed off from the desk. "You could reopen it. Update it, obviously—but there's something here. All this vintage inventory, the party supplies, the ribbons? People love that kind of thing. And the location is great, right off the beach."

"It would be a lot of work."

"It would be," Claire agreed. "But think about it—you've got the infrastructure. The space is here, it's connected to Chipper's, which means foot traffic. You wouldn't have to start from scratch."

Lauren walked back into the main store area, taking in the rows of shelves, the dusty inventory, the potential buried under decades of neglect. "I wouldn't even know where to start. And I'm already running Chipper's full-time—who would actually run the store?"

"That's where I come in," Claire said, following her. "I could help out a couple days a week. Bring my laptop, sit at the counter, work on my design stuff between customers. It would probably be slow at first anyway."

"You want to help out at the store?"

"Why not? I work from home anyway—my schedule's flexible. And I need something to do besides unpack boxes, stare at my laptop, and think about my failed marriage." Claire's tone was light, but Lauren caught the edge underneath. "And honestly? This sounds kind of fun. Like a project we could do together."

"You really think people would actually pay for this stuff?" Lauren asked, looking around at the dusty shelves.

"Are you kidding? People love this retro stuff. It's like a time capsule in here."

Lauren looked at Claire, who was nodding. "But what happens when we sell through it all? There has to be enough here to last at least a year, maybe more, but eventually it'll run out."

Claire walked down one of the aisles, eyeing the packed shelves. "Cross that bridge when you come to it. By then, you'll know if the concept works. Maybe you source more vintage from estate sales and flea markets, or start mixing in new items as the old stuff sells out. The store can evolve."

"I still don't know," Lauren said. But even as she spoke, she felt something shifting inside her—possibility replacing doubt.

Evan pulled out his phone. "I'm going to call Dad and tell him about the store."

Something shifted in Claire's expression, but she just nodded.

Evan stepped toward the front of the store, and Lauren could hear his muffled voice greeting his father. She caught Claire's eye, but neither of them said anything.

Then Evan's voice changed—surprised, confused. "Oh. Um, hi."

Lauren and Claire both looked toward where Evan stood. His phone was pressed to his ear, his expression uncertain.

"I was calling my dad," they heard him say. "Is he there?"

A pause.

"Okay. Yeah. Thanks."

He came back to where they stood, his face carefully neutral. "A woman answered Dad's phone."

Claire had gone completely still. "What did she say?"

"She said he was in the shower and asked if she could take a message." Evan looked at his mother. "Who was that?"

"I don't know," Claire said quietly. "Maybe someone from work?"

But her voice lacked conviction, and Lauren saw the flash of pain cross her face.

"Can I try calling again?" Evan asked.

"Later," Claire said. "Let's go."

Bridget looked up from examining a package of vintage stickers. "What's going on?"

"Nothing," Claire said. "Come on, guys."

They locked up the store and headed back through Chipper's. George and Bobby had finished cleaning and were getting ready to leave.

"See you tomorrow," George called as they headed out the back door.

Lauren walked Claire and the kids out to their car. Claire moved mechanically, helping the kids get settled, not meeting Lauren's eyes.

"You okay?" Lauren asked quietly when Claire finally closed the back door.

"No," Claire said. "But I will be. Eventually."

Lauren squeezed her sister's arm. Claire managed a small nod but kept her gaze on the ground.

"Call me if you need anything," Lauren said. "Seriously. Day or night."

"I know." Claire pulled back, forced a smile. "Go. I'm fine. We're fine."

But as Lauren watched them drive away, she could see Claire's hands gripping the steering wheel, her shoulders tight, looking smaller and more alone than Lauren had ever seen her.

* * *

The Clam Bar in Somers Point was a local institution. Lauren had always loved this place—the casual atmosphere, the excellent food, the counter seating.

She spotted Brenna already at the counter, sitting on one of the padded stools. Brenna waved when she saw her, and Lauren slid onto the stool beside her.

"I got here early and grabbed us a spot," Brenna said, gesturing to the cooler by her feet. "I brought some wine. Hope that's okay."

"More than okay."

The dinner crowd hadn't fully arrived yet, leaving the counter area relatively quiet. A few people sat at tables behind them, and music played softly overhead—classic rock that blended into the background.

"I still can't believe you're here," Brenna said, shaking her head.

"Full-time resident as of last summer." Lauren accepted a glass from the server and poured wine Brenna had brought. "I moved back to help with my grandparents' restaurant and ended up staying. It wasn't the plan, but it worked out."

They ordered—tuna for Brenna, fried oyster platter for Lauren—and settled in to catch up properly. Brenna talked about her years in California, working on kelp forest restoration projects and studying ocean acidification. Her enthusiasm was infectious, the way she described diving in cold Pacific waters and cataloging species changes over time.

"But I missed the East Coast. And when this position opened up at the research center here, it felt perfect. Better funding, interesting projects."

"Where are you living?" Lauren asked.

"I found this tiny apartment a block from the beach. It's basically a studio with delusions of grandeur, but it has a deck with an ocean view, so I'm not complaining." Brenna took a sip of her wine. "What about you? Where are you staying?"

"I bought a house last year," Lauren said. "It's on the bay. Needed a lot of work when I got it, but it's coming together."

Their food arrived, and they ate while Brenna talked about her current projects. She was working with several species along the New Jersey coast, but her main focus right now involved diamondback terrapins.

"They're these incredible turtles that live in the salt marshes," Brenna explained. "They're pretty much the only turtles around here that can handle brackish water full-time. They've got these special adaptations—salt glands, basically—that let them thrive where other turtles can't."

"I don't think I've ever seen one," Lauren admitted.

"Most people haven't. They spend most of their time in the water, and you'd have to be out in the marshes to spot them." Brenna's eyes lit up as she talked. "But they're amazing to work with. Real survivors."

Lauren watched her friend's face brighten. "You really love what you do."

"I do," Brenna said simply. "It's not glamorous, and the pay isn't great, but getting to work with these species, seeing the direct impact of conservation efforts? There's nothing else I'd rather be doing."

Lauren asked about other projects, and Brenna talked about her work with horseshoe crabs, with shorebirds, with the various restoration initiatives happening along the coast. Lauren found herself fascinated by the complexity of it all, the interconnected web of species and habitats that she'd never really thought about before.

"Enough about me," Brenna said, pushing her empty plate aside. "Tell me about you. You're running your family's restaurant, but what else?" She tilted her head. "So what's the deal with Matt? Are you two together?"

"We are," Lauren said, smiling. "Since last summer."

"And how is it?"

"It's good," Lauren said. "He's sweet, funny, easy to be around."

"Does he actually surf? Or just sell the gear?"

"He surfs. Pretty much every day when the waves are good."

"That's very on-brand for Ocean City." Brenna grinned.

Lauren laughed.

"I'm glad you're happy," Brenna added.

"What about you?" Lauren asked. "Are you seeing anyone?"

Brenna shook her head, then she took a sip. "No. I ended things with someone about a year ago. We'd been together for a few years, but we wanted different things."

"I'm sorry," Lauren said.

"Don't be. It was the right call." Brenna paused. "He wanted to settle down, buy a house together, the whole traditional thing. And I just... wasn't there. I wanted to focus on my career, take this job when it came up, have the freedom to move if I needed to." She gave a small, self-deprecating smile. "I know that probably sounds weird for someone in their forties. Most people are building lives by now, not running away from them. But it wasn't fair to either of us to keep pretending we could make it work."

Lauren nodded. "That takes courage, to end something when you know it's not right."

"Or stubbornness," Brenna said with a quiet laugh. "Sometimes I'm not sure which."

Lauren hesitated then said, "Weren't you with that guy Ashton in college?"

Brenna smiled, a little wistful. "I was. Wow, I haven't thought about him in a while." Her expression warmed. "He was my first love. I thought he was the one."

Lauren leaned forward. "What happened?"

"We were just too young, I think. Being pulled in different directions. He wanted to go to grad school in Chicago, I got that marine biology fellowship in California. We tried long distance for a bit, but..." She shrugged. "It just didn't work out. I wonder what he's up to these days."

They ordered another round and talked until the dinner crowd started filling in around them, forcing them to speak louder over the increasing noise. They exchanged more stories from college, laughed about professors they'd had and parties they'd attended, reminisced about that terrible apartment they'd shared with the bathroom that was always mysteriously wet.

"We should do this again," Brenna said as they paid their bill. "I'm here for the foreseeable future, and it would be nice to have friends outside of work."

"Absolutely," Lauren said.

CHAPTER FIVE

Maddie spotted the crowd from half a block away.

People clustered on the boardwalk in front of the arcade, more than she'd expect for nine in the morning in mid-May. Her stomach dropped as she quickened her pace, the paint supplies in her canvas bag bouncing against her hip.

She'd headed out this morning determined to get a solid three hours of work in before the afternoon heat made the lift unbearable. The mural was coming together beautifully—the wave now had depth and movement, the sky gradient exactly the shade she'd envisioned. She was just days away from finishing.

But as she got closer and the crowd came into clearer focus, something felt wrong. A shop owner from the salt water taffy store stood with his arms crossed, shaking his head. Two women pointed at the wall, one with her hand over her mouth. Tyler from the fry stand was there too, his usually easygoing expression replaced with something that looked like anger.

Maddie's pace slowed. Her heart began to pound.

She pushed through the small gathering, muttering, "Excuse me," until she was close enough to see the damage.

The air left her lungs.

Red spray paint slashed across the wave she'd spent days perfecting. Crude letters spelled out words she couldn't quite process, her vision tunneling. Someone had drawn over the meticulously layered blues and whites with thick, dripping paint. The delicate translucence of the water was obliterated. The crest of the wave—the part she'd been most proud of— was barely visible under the vandalism.

"Maddie." Tyler's voice came from beside her. "I'm so sorry. I called Steve—he's on his way."

She couldn't speak. Her throat had closed up entirely. She just stared at the wall, at the destruction of weeks of work, at the mockery someone had made of her art.

"This is awful," one of the women said. "Who would do something like this?"

"Bored teenagers, probably," the salt water taffy shop owner offered.

She walked away from the crowd on shaking legs, her vision blurring. She made it to a bench and sat down, pulling her paint supplies bag close. Her hands still trembled.

Tyler came over after a few minutes. "You alright?"

Maddie nodded, not trusting her voice.

"Steve should be here soon." Tyler glanced toward the boardwalk.

"Thanks for doing that."

She watched the boardwalk activity around her—tourists and locals heading to shops, people already claiming spots on the beach. Normal morning routine. But she felt like she was watching it all from underwater.

Tyler was quiet for a moment before speaking. "Everyone on the boardwalk has been talking about how beautiful the mural was looking. Is looking," he corrected quickly. "You'll fix it."

Maddie looked back at the wall, blinking hard.

The arcade owner arrived, a middle-aged man in khakis and a polo shirt, his face flushed. "I got here as fast as I could.

Tyler called me—" He stopped short when he saw the wall. "Oh no. Oh, Maddie, I'm so sorry."

"Thanks for coming, Steve," Maddie managed.

Steve immediately pulled out his phone. "I'm calling the police. This is criminal damage. They need to file a report."

She was grateful someone else was taking charge. She felt frozen, unable to do much more than stare at the ruined sections of her work.

Steve paused, phone halfway to his ear. "I wish I had cameras on this side of the building. I should have thought of that from the start."

The salt water taffy store owner, who'd been standing nearby, spoke up. "My camera only covers my front entrance. Doesn't point this way at all."

"It must've happened overnight," Tyler said. "I closed up around eleven, and it wasn't like this then."

Steve finished his call. "The police are sending someone. They said it'll be about forty minutes—they're dealing with a fender bender on Ninth Street."

Maddie sighed. It was going to be a long morning.

"I want you to know," Steve said, "that I still want you to finish the mural. However long it takes to fix this, whatever materials you need—I'm covering it. We're not letting whoever did this win."

Relief flooded through Maddie. She'd been bracing herself for Steve to say it was too much trouble, that he'd just paint over the whole thing. "Really?"

"Really. In fact, I'm going to put up a security camera on this side of the building today." Steve's eyes lingered on the vandalism. "I'm sorry this happened. But we're going to make it right."

A few of the other shop owners approached, offering their support. The woman from the bookstore two doors down squeezed Maddie's shoulder. "We've all been watching it come together. It's been the talk of the boardwalk. Don't let this discourage you."

"Everyone loves what you're doing," the salt water taffy store owner added. "My customers ask about it every day."

Their kindness made her eyes sting. She managed to thank them before they headed back to their shops, leaving her alone with Tyler and Steve.

After Steve headed back to the arcade, the adrenaline was wearing off, leaving Maddie exhausted. She pulled out her water bottle and took a long drink.

Tyler stayed with her while she sat there processing.

Maddie forced herself to look at the wall again. Really look at it. The spray paint had soaked into her carefully applied layers. The red was garish against the blues, and whoever had done this had been thorough. They'd targeted the sections that had taken her the longest to perfect.

"I can't believe someone would do this," she said. "I keep trying to understand it. Was it personal? Random? Were they drunk and thought it would be funny?"

"I doubt it was personal," Tyler said. "Your mural's been nothing but positive attention for the boardwalk. People love it."

Maddie took a sip of water. "It's fixable, right? I'm not crazy for thinking I can salvage this?"

"You can definitely salvage it," Tyler said. "It'll take some work, but you're talented. You'll make it work." He glanced back toward his stand, where a small line was starting to form. "I should get back and help out. My coworker's been handling things, but it's getting busy. If you need anything, just come find me, okay?"

"Thanks, Tyler. I appreciate you staying with me."

He gave her a small wave before heading back to the fry stand.

The police arrived thirty minutes later. Steve came back out to meet them, and Maddie gave her statement, provided photos of the mural before the vandalism, and watched as they took pictures of the damage. They were sympathetic but realistic—without security footage or witnesses, the chances of finding who did it were slim.

After they left, Maddie stood in front of the wall one more time. The morning sun made the vandalism impossible to ignore. What had taken her weeks to build—layer after careful layer—someone had destroyed in minutes. She could see where they'd worked fast, the spray paint running in some spots, uneven and careless in others.

But it wasn't ruined. It was vandalized. And vandalism could be undone.

Maddie pulled out her phone and opened her notes app, starting a list: primer, new paint to match the original colors. She'd have to take her time, but she could make it work.

She gathered her paint supplies and headed back toward the gallery. As she walked, she called Dominic.

He answered on the first ring. "Hey, I was just thinking about you. Want me to bring lunch by later?"

"Someone vandalized the mural," Maddie said, her voice steadier than she expected.

Silence. Then: "What? When?"

"Overnight, sometime after eleven. I got here this morning, and it was covered in spray paint."

"Are you okay?" His voice had shifted, concerned but calm. "Where are you?"

"I'm heading back to the gallery now. The police came, took a statement. Steve—the arcade owner—he's still letting me finish it. He's even putting up cameras."

"That's good. That's really good." She could hear the sounds of the pizza shop in the background—oven doors, metal clanging. "Do you need anything?"

"No, I'm okay. I just... wanted to tell you. I'm going to regroup and get started on the repairs."

"You've got this," Dominic said, and there was such

certainty in his voice that Maddie felt herself relax a little. "I know you do. Let me know if you need an extra set of hands. I'll help however I can."

"Thanks, Dom."

"I mean it. Whatever you need."

After they hung up, Maddie continued walking. She looked back once at where the mural stood, way in the distance now. She had to squint to make it out among the other buildings.

She'd fix it. Somehow.

* * *

Matt's shoulder protested as he went through his warm-up routine, rotating his arm in slow circles. The makeshift pitching area he'd set up in his backyard was basic—a pitching net with a strike zone target, and a bucket of baseballs he'd bought from a sporting goods store.

The bay stretched out to his left, the water flat and still. A few boats bobbed at their moorings, and somewhere in the neighborhood a dog barked. His backyard was private, bordered by hedges on one side and Lauren's property on the other. Scout, his cat, sat at the screen door, watching him with mild interest, tail twitching occasionally.

He'd measured it out carefully—sixty feet, six inches from the mound to the target. Regulation distance. No point in practicing if he wasn't going to do it right.

Matt picked up a ball. The stakes couldn't be lower—this was beer league, not a career. But his heart rate still picked up as he stepped onto the mound.

He went into his windup—a motion his body remembered even if his mind questioned every movement. Left leg up, hands together, step toward home, release.

The ball sailed high and right, hitting the net well above the strike zone.

"Well," Matt muttered to himself. "That's a start."

He threw again. Better, but still outside. The third caught the corner. The fourth was closer—middle of the zone, though it had no velocity.

His shoulder was already beginning to burn.

Matt forced himself to keep going, throwing methodically. He started with fastballs—his bread and butter back in the day. Some found the general area of the strike zone. Most didn't. He tried a few changeups, but they felt awkward, his timing off. Every throw reminded him how far he'd fallen from the player he used to be.

But there were moments—fleeting moments—when muscle memory took over and the ball went where he wanted it to go. When his arm followed through smoothly and the tension eased. Those moments made him keep throwing, even as sweat soaked through his shirt and his arm grew heavier.

He was collecting balls from the net when he heard a gate click. Matt looked up to see Lauren walking through from her yard, wearing cutoff shorts and a tank top, her hair pulled back in a ponytail.

"Hey," she called. "I heard the thunking and came to investigate."

"Sorry if I'm being loud." Matt tossed another ball into the bucket.

"You're not loud. I was just curious." Lauren walked closer, taking in the setup—the pitching net, the bucket of balls. "You're practicing."

"Attempting to practice," Matt corrected with a smile. "Key word being 'attempting.'"

"Can I watch?"

He hesitated. The idea of Lauren witnessing how bad he was at this felt suddenly vulnerable. She'd never known him as the baseball player. She knew him as the guy who ran a surf shop, who'd grown up in Ocean City—not the version of him that used to take the mound.

But she was looking at him with genuine interest, not judgment, so he nodded. "Sure. Fair warning, though—I'm terrible."

"I doubt that."

"Watch and learn."

Lauren settled onto the small bench near the back door, drawing her knees up. Matt walked back to the mound, trying to ignore the fact that she was there. He grabbed a ball, went through his motion, and released.

The ball hit the net at chest level, just outside the zone.

"That looked good to me," Lauren offered.

"That would have been ball one," Matt said, grabbing another ball. "I was aiming middle-middle."

He threw again. This one was better—caught the bottom of the zone, though it had no movement whatsoever. Just a straight fastball, probably topping out somewhere between sixty-five and seventy if he had to guess.

"How long has it been since you pitched?" Lauren asked.

"Competitively? Twenty years, give or take. At the field the other night I only managed a couple dozen pitches before my arm gave out." He flexed his fingers, feeling the familiar tightness starting to build. "Already past that today."

"Does it hurt?"

"Not the way it used to," Matt said. "After the surgery, for years, it hurt constantly. Even just reaching for something off a high shelf would send this shooting pain down my arm. But that eventually faded. Now it's more like... tightness. Fatigue. A reminder that it's not what it once was."

His next pitch went wide. Lauren didn't comment, just watched with focused attention. There was something about the way she looked at him that made Matt acutely aware of his body—the motion of his arm, the follow-through, the way he planted his back foot.

"How's the store coming?" Matt asked between throws.

"Claire and I are trying to get it sorted out, see if we can even open it." Lauren shifted on the bench. "We found all these old photos and logbooks from when my grandparents ran it. Supplier lists, notes about regular customers. It's like stepping back in time."

"That's pretty cool, though."

"It is. Just overwhelming." She smiled. "But that's tomorrow's problem. Back to pitching."

Matt picked up another ball.

"I've never seen you like this," Lauren said after a few more throws.

"Like what?"

"Like a baseball player." She gestured vaguely. "You always seem so casual, you know? Running the shop, hanging out on the beach. But this—" She paused, her eyes following the line of his throwing arm. "More focused. Athletic. It's nice to watch."

A smile tugged at Matt's lips, something pleasant settling in his chest. His next throw found the middle of the target with something approaching his old form.

"There you go," Lauren said, her face lighting up. "That was perfect."

"That was acceptable," Matt corrected, but he was smiling too.

He worked through the rest of the bucket, fatigue building but manageable. When he finally set down the last ball, exhaustion radiated down his arm.

"You're worried about re-injuring it," Lauren said. It wasn't a question.

Matt walked over and sat down beside her on the bench. "Yeah. I mean, logically I know this is different. I'm not trying to throw ninety-five anymore. I'm not pitching every fifth day on three days' rest. I'm throwing a fraction of what I used to. The risk should be minimal."

"But?"

"But it's the same shoulder. The same injury. And I remember what it felt like when it gave out the first time—like something tearing deep inside, this pop that I felt more than heard." He opened and closed his fist. "I know what I'm risking every time I throw a pitch. That's always going to be there."

Lauren was quiet for a moment. "Is it worth it? The risk?"

"I don't know yet," Matt admitted. "Ask me in a few weeks when I'm either pitching in actual games or sitting in a doctor's office being told I'm an idiot."

"You're not an idiot," Lauren said. "You're just trying to do something you love again. There's nothing wrong with that."

"When did you get so wise?"

"I've always been wise. You just weren't paying attention."

He laughed, nudging her shoulder with his. "Fair point."

His shoulder throbbed, already protesting the practice session. Tomorrow it would be worse—stiff and sore, a testament to his limitations. But sitting here with Lauren, the taste of salt in the air and the sound of water nearby, he thought maybe she was right.

Maybe some things were worth the risk.

CHAPTER SIX

The binoculars had become a permanent fixture in Nancy's car. They lived in the center console now, right next to Joe's sunglasses and the bird field guide they'd picked up at the bookstore, ready for whenever they decided to stop at the Welcome Center on their way back from the mainland.

"Should we?" Joe asked as they approached the bridge.

"Absolutely," Nancy said, already putting on her turn signal.

It had only been a few days since their first visit, but Nancy had been thinking about the rookery constantly. She wanted to see the ibis chicks again, check on the nests, watch the birds coming and going. See if more eggs had hatched.

Nancy pulled into the parking lot and cut the engine. Joe was already reaching for the binoculars before she'd even unbuckled her seatbelt.

They headed straight for the railing. Below them, the trees stretched out across the marsh, and there—dotting the branches—were the white shapes of the birds.

"Look how many there are," Nancy said, leaning against the railing. "More than before."

Joe raised the binoculars first. "Oh man. Nancy, you've got to see this."

She took them from him, adjusting the focus. The birds came into view—egrets perched on nests, necks arched over eggs or small gray chicks. She could see one adult standing guard while its mate flew in with nesting material. Another egret preened on a nearby branch, smoothing its feathers with its beak.

"There," Joe said, pointing to a tree on the left side of the colony. "That's the nest we saw last time. The one with the white ibis."

Nancy found it in the binoculars. The adult ibis was there, feeding the two small chicks. They looked more alert than before, their heads bobbing as they begged for food.

"They're growing," Nancy said softly. "Look at them."

They took turns with the binoculars, watching the constant motion of the rookery. An egret landed at its nest and lowered its head to feed the chicks, which immediately crowded around, clamoring. Another pair seemed to be negotiating territory, their necks extending in what looked like a ritualized dance. The sound drifted up from the rookery—a chorus of squawks and calls, the rush of wings.

Nancy lowered the binoculars to give her eyes a rest and glanced at the sky. Something had changed since they'd arrived. The blue overhead had dulled to a flat gray, and in the distance, toward the mainland, darker clouds were building.

"Joe," she said. "Look at that."

He followed her gaze. "Storm coming in."

Nancy checked her phone. The radar showed a band of storms moving across South Jersey, heading straight for the coast. Heavy rain, the forecast said. Possible thunder.

"Just a few more minutes," Joe said. "I want to watch that heron a bit longer."

They stayed at the railing, watching. The birds seemed unaware of the approaching storm, or maybe they simply didn't care. They continued their routines—coming and going, feeding, tending nests. The wind picked up slightly, ruffling their feathers, but they adjusted their positions and held firm.

Then everything changed.

The hawk came from nowhere—a dark shape plummeting from the sky, wings pulled back as it dove toward the rookery. Nancy didn't even have time to raise the binoculars before it struck.

"Whoa," Joe said.

The hawk hit one of the nests near the top of the colony, talons extended, going for the chicks. The egret parent was on it instantly, wings spread wide, neck jabbing forward with its sharp beak.

The entire rookery erupted in alarm. Birds called out, sharp and frantic, while parents hunkered lower over their nests. The hawk tried to grab whatever it had come for—an egg, a chick, Nancy couldn't tell—but the defending egret was relentless.

Nancy's heart hammered in her chest. Through the binoculars, she could see the violence of it—the hawk's talons grasping, the egret stabbing with its beak, feathers floating in the air. The sound rose up to them, harsh cries that were nothing like the pleasant calls from moments before.

"Come on," Joe muttered. "Get out of there."

It was hard to tell who he was rooting for—the hawk trying to feed itself, or the egret defending its young. Both were just trying to survive.

The hawk broke away suddenly, launching itself back into the air empty-taloned. It circled once, as if considering another attempt, then banked hard and disappeared toward the mainland. The defending egret lowered itself back over its nest.

The other birds in the rookery began to calm, though their agitation was still visible in the way they moved on their nests, alert, watching the sky.

"Did it get anything?" Nancy asked.

"I don't think so," Joe said. "It fought it off."

Nancy felt something wet hit her arm. She looked up just as the first raindrops began to fall, fat and heavy, spattering against the railing. The sky had darkened considerably while they'd been watching the attack, the storm clouds rolling in faster than she'd expected.

"We should probably go," she said, but made no move toward the car.

The rain picked up, steady now but not yet heavy. In the rookery, the birds were already responding. Parents pressed lower over their nests, extending their wings to create shelters. Some shifted, tucking themselves more firmly over their eggs. One egret shook its head as rain hit its face, then held its position.

"They're staying put," Joe said quietly. "They're not going anywhere."

The wind kicked up, swaying the trees where the birds nested, branches dipping and rising. Thunder rumbled in the distance. The rain intensified, going from steady to heavy in seconds.

"Okay, now we really need to go," Nancy said.

"Nancy, come on," Joe said, grabbing her hand. "We're getting soaked."

They ran for the car, rain plastering Nancy's hair to her head. She fumbled with the door, finally getting it open and diving inside. Joe scrambled into the passenger seat, both of them breathing hard.

Nancy started the engine and pulled out of the parking lot, windshield wipers working frantically against the downpour. Rain drummed on the roof as they drove back toward Ocean City.

"That was intense," Joe said.

"Yeah," Nancy agreed. "Intense and exhilarating."

* * *

Lauren stood in the center of the store, hands on her hips, surveying the work ahead of them. They'd been at it for an hour already, and they'd barely made a dent.

Rain drummed steadily on the roof. The storm that had blown in earlier showed no signs of letting up.

"Okay," she said to Claire, who was wiping dust from a shelf of vintage beach pails. "We need a system. This is too overwhelming otherwise."

Claire straightened up, pushing hair out of her face and leaving a streak of dust across her forehead. "Agreed. What are you thinking?"

"Section by section," Lauren said. "We clean one area completely, catalog what we have, figure out fair prices. The old tags are still on everything, but we need to reprice for today's market. Not crazy high, but what makes sense."

"Good plan."

Bridget and Evan wandered off to explore while Lauren and Claire got to work. Lauren could hear them moving through the aisles, occasionally calling out discoveries—"Look at these old pencils with the designs!" "Check out this beach ball, it's huge!"—but they kept to themselves, absorbed in their own treasure hunt through the decades-old inventory.

They started with the party supply section. Lauren pulled down a package of E.T. paper plates, the cellophane yellowed with age, the price tag showing two dollars and fifty cents.

"How much do you think we should charge for these?" she asked Claire.

Claire examined the package then pulled out her phone. "Let me see what these are going for." She typed for a moment, then her eyes widened. "Whoa. These are selling for sixty dollars on eBay."

"Sixty dollars?" Lauren said. "For paper plates?"

"Unopened vintage E.T. supplies," Claire said, reading from her screen. "Still sealed in the original packaging."

"We can't charge eBay prices in a beach town store,"

Lauren said. "Nobody's paying sixty dollars for paper plates on impulse."

"No, but we could do twenty, maybe thirty? Still way more than the original price." Claire took the package from Lauren, examining it with new appreciation. "The really valuable stuff we can sell online to collectors. But even at half the eBay price, we're sitting on more than we thought."

They worked methodically through the section, uncovering packages of Ghostbusters napkins, Strawberry Shortcake tablecloths, He-Man party favors. Each time they found something particularly interesting, Claire would look it up online and report back with values that made Lauren's head spin.

"This is insane," Lauren said, writing down prices in a notebook. "Some of this stuff is worth more now than when it was new."

Claire nodded. "That's how collectibles work. Scarcity and nostalgia."

The rain intensified, pounding harder against the roof. Thunder rumbled, closer now.

From somewhere in the back of the store, they could hear Bridget and Evan's voices, talking excitedly about something they'd found. Lauren smiled, remembering her own childhood explorations in this place.

The storm was at its peak now. Rain hammered against the building, and the lights flickered once before steadying.

"Hey," Evan called from the back corner near the office. "There's a door here."

Lauren made her way over. Sure enough, partially hidden behind a tall shelving unit, was a door she'd never noticed before. It was painted the same color as the wall, easy to miss if you weren't looking for it.

"Is it locked?" Claire asked, joining them.

Evan tried the handle. "Yeah."

Lauren went back to the office area, digging through the desk drawers until she found a small metal box filled with keys.

Most were labeled—cash register, front door, supply closet—but one had no label at all. She brought it back and tried it in the lock.

The lock turned with a click.

"Okay, that's kind of exciting," Claire said.

Lauren pushed the door open. It was dark inside, and she felt along the wall for a light switch. She flipped it, but nothing happened.

"Dead bulb," Claire said.

"Use your phone," Evan suggested, already turning on his flashlight.

They all pulled out their phones, the beams cutting through the darkness of the storage room. It was larger than Lauren expected—maybe twenty by twenty-five feet—and as the light swept across the space, they could see shelves filled with boxes.

"Wow," Bridget breathed.

Like everything else in the store, the boxes were covered in a thick layer of dust from decades locked away.

Lauren spotted a desk lamp in the corner and walked over to it, clicking it on. It illuminated instantly, casting a warm glow across the room.

"Much better," she said, setting her phone aside.

She stepped closer to the shelves, reading the labels on the boxes. "Promotional displays. Limited edition. Special order."

She pulled down the nearest box, setting it on a small table nearby. The tape was old but still sealed. She broke it open and lifted the flaps.

Inside, nestled in newspaper from 1989, were retail boxes. Pyrex boxes with the original price stickers still attached. She lifted one out carefully—a boxed set that had never been opened. She broke the seal and opened it, revealing mixing bowls in pristine condition, nested together. The distinctive turquoise color gleamed under the lamp light, decorated with an intricate pattern of white butterprint designs showing an Amish couple with farm animals.

"These are Pyrex bowls," Claire said, moving closer. "But why would they have vintage Pyrex? This pattern looks like it's from the fifties or sixties."

Lauren looked at the box more carefully. A shipping label showed it had been purchased from an estate sale company in 1987. "I think they bought out old inventory from other stores and sales. Look at this label."

Lightning flashed, visible even through the small window in the storage room. Thunder followed almost immediately, loud enough to make them all jump.

"No way," Bridget said, peering into the box. "Are those worth anything?"

Claire was already on her phone, typing frantically. She let out a low whistle as she scrolled through results. "The turquoise Butterprint pattern? These are really collectible. A full set in original packaging could be worth several hundred dollars. Maybe more."

Lauren looked back at the shelf where she'd found the first box. There were at least a dozen more boxes of the same Butterprint pattern stacked behind it, filling two entire shelves. And beyond those, she could see other Pyrex patterns—boxes labeled with names like "Pink Gooseberry," "Snowflake," and "Primary Colors"—that she hadn't even examined yet.

They opened another box. This one was labeled "Kitchen —Estate Purchase 1985" and contained CorningWare casserole dishes in the Blue Cornflower pattern, each piece still wrapped in its original packaging with price tags from another era. Lauren counted at least fifteen boxes of various Corning-Ware patterns—Blue Cornflower, Spice of Life, Wildflower— stacked on multiple shelves. Another set held Fire King jadeite dishes—that distinctive green milk glass that collectors went crazy for—and behind it, a full section of shelving was dedicated to Fire King in different styles and sizes, easily twenty or more cartons. A fourth container held vintage Tupperware sealed in its original packaging, the colors vibrant and the plastic unblemished by age. The Tupperware had its own shelving unit with what looked like dozens of sets.

Claire surveyed the room. "But why buy all this if they weren't going to sell it?"

Lauren thought about it, glancing at box after box of carefully stored vintage kitchenware. "Maybe they were going to expand the store? Or pivot to selling vintage housewares alongside the party supplies? Or maybe they saw these as investments—buy low at estate sales, hold onto them, sell high later."

"Or maybe they just never got around to it," Claire said quietly.

Against the far wall, Lauren found a box that made her stop entirely. Inside were pieces of Pyrex in patterns she'd never seen before—a pink pattern with hearts and shamrocks that looked almost too delicate to be real.

"Claire," she said, her voice barely above a whisper. "Come look at this."

Claire peered inside. "What pattern is that?"

Lauren was already searching on her phone. When the results loaded, she had to read them twice to believe what she was seeing. "It's called Lucky in Love. It's one of the rarest Pyrex patterns ever made. Only produced in 1959."

"How much?" Claire asked.

"One casserole dish in this pattern sold at auction for almost six thousand dollars."

They stared at the set, which contained not just one piece but four different pieces of the Lucky in Love pattern, all in pristine condition.

"Unbelievable," Claire said under her breath, then turned to scan the shelves. "Lauren, look."

She pointed to a section of shelving that held at least eight more boxes, all with the same shipping label and date. All Lucky in Love. Lauren felt her heart race as she did the math in her head.

"This changes everything," Lauren said, sinking onto an

old folding chair near the table. "The inventory out front is valuable enough. But this room..." She gestured around at the shelves. "This is serious money." She paused, thinking. "I can finally do this. All this vintage inventory, the original fixtures—it's like a time capsule. I just need to clean everything, reprice for today's market, and open the doors. The appeal is the nostalgia, the rare stuff that's hard to find these days."

"A preserved store from another era," Claire said, nodding slowly as the possibilities dawned on her. "And once the dead-stock sells through, you'll figure out what comes next."

"Right. So the work isn't that overwhelming—mostly cleaning and pricing. We can have it ready in less than a week."

In the back corner of the room, beyond all the containers of kitchenware, Lauren noticed something else. An old employee break room setup—a small table with two chairs, a coffee pot still sitting on a hot plate, mugs with long-dried coffee stains around the rims. A calendar on the wall showed November 1996, the last month the store had been open. Someone had circled the date November 28th and written "Thanksgiving" in neat script.

"Look at this," she murmured.

Claire came over. "It's like they just stepped out for a minute."

On the table was a newspaper, folded open to the crossword puzzle. Someone had filled in half the answers in pencil. A jacket hung on the back of one chair, a faded name tag still pinned to the lapel.

"This is like a museum," Claire said, taking in the room with wonder.

They spent another hour carefully documenting what they'd found in the storage room before finally heading back out to the main store. The regular inventory seemed almost mundane now in comparison.

The rain had stopped. The storm had passed while they'd been absorbed in their discovery.

"We should probably call it a day," Claire said, looking at her phone. "It's almost five."

Lauren looked around at what they'd accomplished. One section of party supplies cleaned and cataloged. The storage room discovered and partially inventoried. It didn't seem like much compared to the enormity of the task ahead, but it was a start.

As they locked up and headed out through Chipper's, Lauren felt a mixture of excitement and trepidation. They'd uncovered something significant today—not just valuable inventory, but a glimpse into her grandparents' business sense and planning. The store had been waiting all these years, holding its secrets, ready for someone to find them again.

CHAPTER SEVEN

The salt marsh stretched out in every direction, a tapestry of green cordgrass rippling in the breeze off the bay. Brenna stood knee-deep in brackish water, the mud sucking at her rubber boots with each step, and felt completely at peace.

This was her element. Not the air-conditioned lab back at the research center, not the boardroom where she presented findings to township councils. Out here, where land and water merged into something neither solid nor liquid, where the ecosystem breathed and shifted with the tides—this was where she belonged.

"Over here!" called Griffin, one of her volunteers, a college kid from Stockton doing an internship. He was twenty yards away, crouched near a tidal creek. "I think I found one!"

Brenna made her way over, stepping carefully to avoid disturbing the marsh plants. The cordgrass grew thick here, its roots forming a complex network that held the entire ecosystem together. Being out here, surrounded by the living marsh, reminded her why she'd chosen this work. No amount of data or presentations could capture what she felt standing here, watching a great egret pick its way through the shallows, seeing fiddler crabs scatter at her approach.

Griffin held up a diamondback terrapin, its shell streaked with growth rings, its dark-spotted gray head tucked defensively into its shell.

"Female," Brenna said, taking the turtle and examining it. "Look at the size. Males rarely get bigger than five inches. This one's pushing seven."

She pulled out her measuring tape and calipers, calling out numbers for Alice, her other volunteer, to record. Shell length, width, weight. She checked for tags or notches from previous captures, finding none. With practiced efficiency, she applied a small notch pattern to the marginal scutes—a unique identifier that would let them track this individual if they caught her again.

"Why the notches?" Alice asked, her pen poised over the datasheet.

"We don't tag them like we do with sea turtles. These guys are smaller, and external tags can catch on things in the marsh. The notch pattern is permanent and doesn't interfere with their movement."

Brenna examined the growth rings on the carapace—the top shell. "See these rings? They can give us a rough estimate —she's probably fifteen, maybe twenty years old. Terrapins can live forty years or more if they're lucky."

"If they're lucky," Griffin repeated.

"Exactly." Brenna set the terrapin down at the water's edge and watched her paddle away, disappearing into the murky water with surprising grace. "If they avoid the major threats— crab traps, boat strikes, road mortality. This one's already beaten the odds for two decades."

She straightened up, scanning the marsh. The morning sun was climbing higher, and she could feel sweat starting to form under her long-sleeved shirt despite the breeze. May was nesting season, which meant the females were already making their annual trek from the marsh to higher ground to lay eggs.

Which meant they'd be crossing roads.

Brenna tried not to think about that yet. They had four more transects to survey this morning, and she wanted to enjoy being out here before reality intruded.

They worked their way through the marsh, wading through tidal creeks, pushing aside cordgrass, searching for the distinctive dark-spotted heads of terrapins swimming just below the surface. The work required patience—terrapins were surprisingly good at vanishing into the brackish water, and the marsh itself fought back with every step. Brenna's boots sank six inches into the mud with each movement, and more than once she had to grab onto cordgrass to keep from losing her balance.

Griffin spotted the next one sunning itself on a log. The turtle slipped into the water before he could reach it, but Brenna knew it wouldn't go far. She positioned herself downstream, waiting. Sure enough, the terrapin's head popped up thirty seconds later, and she scooped it into her net.

Another female, even larger than the first. They went through the same routine—measurements, notch pattern recorded. This one had battle scars, old notches on the shell edges that Brenna recognized from previous captures. A survivor.

"This is the third time we've caught this girl," Brenna said, checking her records. "She's at least thirty years old."

"That's incredible," Alice said. "To have survived this long with all the threats they face."

"It is. But look at her shell." Brenna pointed to a section that had been damaged and healed, leaving a rough patch. "Probably from a propeller strike. She got lucky. Most turtles don't."

They caught two more—a male who tried to bite Griffin when he picked him up, and a younger female. The male was feisty, his jaw strong despite his smaller size. Alice had to chase the female through the marsh, nearly falling face-first into the mud when the stubborn turtle kept diving just as she reached for it. The chase took them thirty yards before the turtle finally tired.

Griffin discovered a horseshoe crab the size of a dinner plate, its prehistoric armor gleaming in the light. They stopped to watch a great blue heron spear a killifish, marveling at the bird's patience and precision.

The marsh was alive with sound—the rustle of cordgrass, the splash of fish, the calls of red-winged blackbirds defending territory. Brenna breathed it all in, storing the sensory details for later. On hard days, when the paperwork piled up and the grant applications felt endless, she'd remember mornings like this.

By eleven, the sun had burned away the last of the morning coolness, and Brenna called it. They'd covered their planned survey area, caught four terrapins, and collected solid data. A good morning.

They made their way back to the parking area, peeling off their waders and storing equipment in Brenna's truck. Griffin and Alice were laughing about something, their voices bright with the satisfaction of fieldwork well done.

"Thanks for today," Alice said, pulling off her hat and letting her hair down. "This was amazing."

"You both did great work," Brenna said. "I'll be in touch about the next survey."

As the volunteers drove off, Brenna checked her phone, scrolling through the terrapin mortality report she'd been tracking. Local residents had been emailing her photos and locations of dead terrapins since she'd started the project in March. She'd created a simple online form, made flyers, talked to anyone who would listen about reporting road-killed turtles.

The map on her phone showed seventeen confirmed deaths this season already. Seventeen female terrapins, each one representing thousands of eggs that would never be laid, decades of reproductive potential erased in seconds.

She closed her eyes, took a breath. Then she got in her truck and drove toward the area she'd been dreading.

The stretch of Bay Avenue near Corson's Inlet sat at the edge of the marsh, where the road ran alongside the wetlands before continuing toward the bridge. A faded turtle crossing sign stood at the roadside—a warning that did little to slow the summer traffic. It was a necessary route, she understood that. People needed to get to the beach, to cross to Strathmere and the towns farther south. But the timing was catastrophic.

Female terrapins nested from May through July, leaving the safety of the marsh to find suitable sites in the dunes and disturbed soil above the high tide line. To reach those nesting sites, they had to cross this road.

Brenna pulled over at a wide spot and got out. The marsh stretched to her right, healthy and thriving.

She didn't have to walk far.

The first one was near the shoulder, partially hidden by tall grass. Brenna crouched down, swallowing hard. The carapace was crushed, the shell shattered from the impact. It had been a large female, probably carrying eggs.

She pulled out a small kit from her pocket and carefully examined the remains. Sometimes, if a female had been hit recently enough, the eggs could still be viable. She'd learned to harvest them, incubate them at the research center, release the hatchlings back into the marsh.

But this one had been here at least a day, maybe longer. The sun and ants had done their work.

Brenna moved on, scanning the road edges. Fifty feet later, she found another. Then another. Three terrapins in less than a hundred yards of roadway.

The third one was still alive.

Brenna saw the movement, the weak paddle of a front leg, and her heart lurched. She moved quickly, scooping up the terrapin with gentle hands. The shell was cracked—a spiderweb of fractures across the carapace—but the turtle was alert, its head moving, its eyes clear.

"Okay," Brenna said quietly. "Okay, let's see what we can do."

She carried the terrapin back to her truck, her mind already running through options. The research center didn't have facilities for this kind of injury. She needed a veterinarian, someone who dealt with wildlife, who understood reptiles.

She pulled out her phone and searched, her heart pounding. There—a veterinary clinic on Ninth Street. She called, her words tumbling out as she explained what she had, what she needed.

"Bring her in," the receptionist said. "Dr. Grant's between appointments. He'll take a look."

Fifteen minutes later, Brenna pushed through the door of Ocean City Animal Hospital, a plastic container cradled in her arms. The terrapin inside was still moving, still fighting.

The reception area was surprisingly busy for a weekday. A woman with a cat carrier sat in one corner, a man with a golden retriever in another. The receptionist—a young woman with purple streaks in her hair—beckoned Brenna forward.

"The terrapin?"

"Yes."

"He's finishing up with a patient. He'll be right out."

Brenna sat down, the container on her lap, and tried not to think about the two dead turtles still lying on Bay Avenue, about how many more would die before the season ended, about being one person with a handful of volunteers trying to save a species that faced threats from every direction.

A door opened, and a man emerged with a beagle on a leash. The dog pulled toward the exit, tail wagging, and the man laughed as he tried to keep up.

Then another door opened, and Brenna looked up.

The veterinarian was younger than she expected—maybe early forties—with dark hair that needed a trim and several days' worth of stubble. He wore scrubs that had seen better days, and there was a stethoscope slung around his neck. But it was his eyes that struck her—brown, intelligent, focused as they took her in.

"You're the researcher? With the turtle?"

Brenna stood. "Brenna Groff. Coastal ecologist. I found her on Bay Avenue. Shell fractures, but she's alert."

"I'm Dr. Grant." He moved closer, peering into the container. "Let's take a look in the exam room."

She followed him through a door and into a small, sterile room with an examination table and cabinets full of supplies. He gestured for her to set the container down, then carefully lifted the terrapin out.

His hands were steady, confident. He examined the shell, gently probing the cracks, checking the turtle's reflexes and responses.

"Diamondback terrapin," he said. "We don't usually treat wildlife, but I'll do what I can."

"Thank you," Brenna said. "Most people don't even know they're out there."

He nodded as he continued his work. "But you do."

"People drive right over them without noticing," Brenna said, trying to keep the bitterness from her voice.

He glanced at her, and their eyes held—an understanding, maybe. "You find a lot of these on the roads?"

"Too many. Bay Avenue is a death trap during nesting season. The females cross to reach the dunes, and cars hit them. I'm out there almost every day, finding crushed turtles."

He turned his attention back to the terrapin, his expression growing more serious. "The shell damage is significant, but nothing's displaced. No obvious organ damage from what I can see. If we can stabilize the fractures, keep her hydrated and stress-free, she has a chance."

"Really?" Brenna felt hope bloom in her chest. She'd expected him to say the injuries were too severe, that euthanasia was the kindest option. She'd prepared herself for that conversation.

"Really. I'll need to clean the wounds, apply some epoxy to stabilize the shell, start her on antibiotics. She'll need to stay here for observation for a few days, then you'll need somewhere to keep her while she heals. How's your setup at the research center?"

"We have holding tanks. I can set up a recovery area. Climate control, filtered water system. We used them last year for blue crabs during a study."

"Perfect. I'd say she needs at least six weeks of rehabilitation before release. Maybe longer depending on how it heals." He was already moving, pulling supplies from cabinets. "The key is preventing infection and giving the shell time to knit back together. Turtle shells have blood supply—they're living bone covered by scutes. They can heal remarkably well if we give them the chance."

He started cleaning the wounds, careful and precise. The terrapin barely moved, conserving energy. Smart, Brenna thought. Terrapins were adaptable, resilient.

Brenna watched him work, mesmerized by the care he took, the gentleness of his movements despite the size of his hands. He talked as he worked, asking questions about terrapin biology that showed genuine interest rather than polite conversation. When had she last met someone who actually wanted to understand her research?

"The brackish water adaptation is fascinating," he said, carefully applying epoxy to stabilize the fractures. "Lachrymal salt glands, right? I've read about them but never seen one in action."

"Exactly," Brenna said, warming to the topic. "Modified tear ducts that excrete concentrated salt solution. You can actually see it sometimes—looks like they're crying, but they're just eliminating excess salt."

"Nature's brilliant," he said. He looked up, meeting her

eyes, and Brenna felt the air between them change. "You must see incredible things in your work."

"I do," Brenna said. "Though lately I've been seeing too many dead turtles and not enough live ones."

"You really care about this," he said, glancing up at her.

Brenna shrugged, suddenly self-conscious. "It's my job."

"It's more than that." His voice was certain.

"Wildlife medicine is why I became a vet. Dogs and cats pay the bills, but this—" He gestured to the terrapin. "This is the good stuff."

Something fluttered inside her, something she hadn't felt in a long time. She pushed it aside, focused on the turtle.

"How much do I owe you?"

He waved a hand. "No charge. Consider it my contribution to terrapin conservation. Though if you're doing research, I'd be interested in hearing more about your work sometime."

"I give talks," Brenna said. "At the research center, to community groups. You should come to one."

"I'd like that." He finished the epoxy work, checked it carefully, then filled a syringe. "Just antibiotics to prevent infection," he explained as he administered the injection. Then he set the terrapin in a shallow container with clean water. "She should be okay here for now. I'll call you in a couple days with an update."

"Let me give you my number," Brenna said, reaching for her phone.

They exchanged contact information, and Brenna noticed he entered her name with both her first and last name, added "terrapin researcher" in the notes field. Professional. This was professional.

So why did her pulse quicken when he smiled at her?

"Call me Josh," he said.

"Brenna. But you knew that."

"I did." He walked her to the door. "Try not to let it get to you too much. The road mortality, I mean. You're doing good work. Sometimes that's all we can do."

Brenna nodded, but as she drove back to the research center, she couldn't shake the image of those shattered shells, couldn't stop counting how many more terrapins would die before the season ended.

And she couldn't stop thinking about the vet's hands, steady and sure as they worked to save one small life.

* * *

Claire's house looked different in the early-evening light, more settled somehow. Lauren pulled into the driveway and grabbed the bottle of wine she'd brought.

The front door was open, screen door letting in the breeze.

"In here!" Claire called from the living room.

Lauren found her sister arranging wine glasses on the coffee table. The living room looked better than it had on moving day. Most of the boxes were gone, pictures hung on the walls, the built-in shelves filled with books and decorative items. Claire had always been good at making spaces feel like home.

"Maddie and Brenna should be here any minute," Lauren said, settling onto the couch. "Where are the kids?"

"At Mom and Dad's for the night. They were excited about staying over."

Claire straightened a coaster then moved it back. "I haven't really done the whole 'making new friends' thing in a while."

"You'll be fine. You already met Maddie at the Christmas parade, remember?"

"Barely. We said hello for like two seconds."

"Well, now you'll actually get to know her. And Brenna's really passionate about her work. You'll like her."

A car pulled up outside, then another right behind it.

"That's them," Lauren said, standing.

Maddie came through the door first, her arms full of

snacks. "I brought cheese! And crackers. And apparently I cannot walk into a house empty-handed, so there's also hummus."

Brenna followed, a little tentative. "Hi. Thanks for having me."

"Of course," Claire said, taking the bags from Maddie. "Good to see you again, Maddie. And you must be Brenna—nice to meet you."

They settled in—Maddie in the armchair, Brenna sitting cross-legged on the floor near the fireplace, Claire and Lauren on the couch. Claire poured wine, and the initial awkwardness began to fade.

"So," Maddie said, drawing out the word. "Can we talk about how someone destroyed my mural?"

"Tell us what happened," Brenna said.

Maddie launched into the story, describing how she'd arrived to find her carefully layered work covered in crude red spray paint—slashes and tags across the wave crest and sky gradient she'd spent weeks perfecting. The boardwalk community was rallying around her. The arcade owner had promised security cameras and whatever supplies she needed to fix it.

"But I keep thinking about who would do this," Maddie said, her fingers tight around her glass. "Was it personal? Random? Someone who hates public art? Someone who's jealous?"

"That's awful," Claire said. "Do the police have any leads?"

"Not really. They took a report, but without witnesses or cameras..." Maddie shrugged. "That's what everyone keeps saying—that it's probably random. But it felt targeted, you know? They hit the sections I'd spent the most time on. Like they knew exactly where to do the most damage."

"Do you have any enemies?" Brenna asked, then immediately shook her head. "Sorry, that sounds dramatic. But is there anyone in Ocean City who might have a problem with you?"

Maddie considered. "Not that I can think of. I keep to

myself mostly—the gallery, the mural, Dominic. I haven't had any conflicts with anyone."

"What about competing artists?" Lauren suggested. "Anyone who might have wanted that commission?"

"Steve, the arcade owner, didn't commission anyone else. He came straight to me." Maddie took a sip of wine. "Though I guess someone could have heard about it and gotten bitter. But bitter enough to trash it? That seems extreme."

They batted around theories for a while—disgruntled artists, teenagers, someone with a grudge against the arcade owner. None of it quite fit.

"The worst part," Maddie said finally, "is not knowing. If it was random, fine. I can accept that. But if someone targeted me specifically..." She trailed off.

Claire reached over and refilled Maddie's glass. "Either way, you're going to fix it. And it's going to be beautiful. Don't let whoever did this win."

Lauren turned to Brenna. "How's the terrapin research going?"

Brenna's expression brightened then clouded. "We had a great morning in the marsh. Caught four terrapins, all healthy. Got some good data."

"But?" Lauren prompted.

"But then I went out to the road by Corson's Inlet." Brenna set down her glass. "Two dead females in less than a hundred yards. Both crushed. A third was still alive, barely. I took her to a vet, and he thinks he can save her, but—" Her voice cracked slightly. "I can't save them all. I can't stop every car. And nesting season is just starting."

The room had gone quiet.

"How many die every year?" Claire asked softly.

"There's been some tracking over the years, but nothing comprehensive or consistent. I set up an online form to make it easier for people to report, and the numbers are worse than I expected. Dozens already this season just in this area. And each female can lay multiple clutches per season, up to twelve eggs per clutch. The reproductive loss is staggering."

"What can be done?" Lauren asked.

Brenna shrugged. "Long term? We need barriers to guide turtles under the road instead of across it. Culverts, maybe. Or wildlife crossings. But that requires township approval, funding, construction. Short term?" She laughed without humor. "I pick up dead turtles and try to save their eggs. I document mortality and hope someone in power eventually cares enough to do something."

"That sounds incredibly depressing," Maddie said.

"It is. But it's also the work. Someone has to do it." Brenna picked up her glass again. "The vet who helped me today, Josh —he was amazing with her. Gentle, knowledgeable. And he didn't charge me anything. Said he'd call when he has an update."

"Wait." Maddie sat forward. "Back up. The vet. Is he cute?"

Brenna's cheeks flushed. "I didn't notice."

"You noticed," Claire said, grinning. "What's he look like?"

"I don't know. Tall. Dark hair. Scruff. He was wearing scrubs."

"And?" Maddie prompted.

"And nothing. He was professional. I was professional."

"But you thought he was attractive," Lauren said.

"I thought he was competent." Brenna took a long sip of wine. "Which is attractive in its own way, I guess. But I'm not looking for anything. I'm still getting settled here. I'm focused on my work."

"Uh huh," Maddie said, clearly unconvinced. "So when he calls about the turtle, are you going to ask him out?"

"No!"

"Why not?"

"Because he's a veterinarian who helped me with a research animal. It would be unprofessional."

"It would be coffee," Claire corrected. "Coffee is not unprofessional."

Brenna shook her head, but she was smiling now. "Can we talk about someone else's love life, please?"

"Fine," Maddie said. "Lauren, how's Matt?"

Lauren felt her face get hot. "Matt's good. Great, actually."

"That's a very satisfied smile," Claire observed.

"He joined a beer league baseball team," Lauren said. "And watching him pitch is..." She fanned herself. "Let's just say athletes are very attractive."

"You think he's hot when he pitches," Maddie said, grinning.

Lauren nodded, laughing. "The focus, the athleticism, the uniform—it's a whole thing."

"Good for you," Claire said.

The conversation drifted, wine flowed, and Lauren felt herself relaxing into the easy rhythm of female friendship. They talked about Maddie's relationship with Dominic, how it had evolved from antagonism to something genuine.

They ended up on the screened porch, watching the sun sink lower. The sound of waves was constant, punctuated by seagulls and distant voices from the beach.

"So," Lauren said carefully, turning to Claire. "How are you really doing? With the separation?"

Claire was quiet for a long moment. The wine had loosened something in her, or maybe it was just the safety of these women, this space.

"I don't know," she said finally. "Some days I'm relieved. Other days I'm terrified. Most days I'm just tired." She took a sip. "And then there's the whole thing with the woman answering Brian's phone when Evan called."

The porch went silent.

"Wait, what?" Maddie said.

"A woman answered Brian's phone. Said he was in the shower, asked if she could take a message." Claire's voice was flat, carefully controlled. "Evan didn't know what to say, so he just said thanks and hung up."

"That's a lot," Brenna said quietly.

"Did you ask Brian about it?" Maddie asked.

"No. What would I say? We're separated. He can see whoever he wants." Claire set down her glass. "But the kids don't need to know that yet. They don't need to know their dad already has someone else in his life."

"Unless he had someone else before," Lauren said quietly.

Claire looked at her sister. "I've thought about that. About whether there was someone the whole time, whether the job falling through was convenient timing. But I'll drive myself crazy wondering. So I'm choosing not to wonder."

"That takes strength," Brenna said.

"Or cowardice," Claire said. "I'm not sure which."

They sat with that for a while, the shadows lengthening across the yard.

"What about the store?" Claire asked finally, clearly ready to change the subject. "Are we really opening in five days?"

Lauren had been trying not to think about that. "I think so? We've cleaned most of the main floor, repriced the party supplies section. We're still figuring out what to do with all the vintage Pyrex and kitchenware from the storage room, but the deadstock inventory on the floor—we just need to open the doors."

"Do you have enough help?" Brenna asked.

"Claire's going to work the counter when she can. I'll be there after breakfast shifts. We're keeping it simple—just opening Thursday through Sunday to start, one to five. See how it goes."

"It's going to be incredible," Maddie said. "People are going to go crazy for vintage items like this. Trust me."

"I hope so." Lauren leaned back in her chair. "What if nobody comes?"

"They'll come," Claire said firmly.

The sky had turned deep purple, stars beginning to emerge. Someone's outdoor speakers were playing music, drifting on the breeze. A perfect Ocean City evening.

"We should do this more often," Brenna said. "This. Getting together, talking."

"Agreed," Maddie said. "Though maybe next time with less collective trauma to process."

"We're women in our forties," Claire said. "There's always trauma to process."

They laughed, and gratitude settled over Lauren.

CHAPTER EIGHT

The afternoon rush at Jungle Surf had finally died down around four thirty. In the last hour, Matt had sold half a dozen rash guards, four pairs of board shorts, a wetsuit, and spent twenty minutes explaining to a tourist from Ohio why you couldn't surf in Ocean City the way you could in Hawaii.

"The waves just aren't big enough here," Matt had explained patiently. "It's more about timing and reading the ocean than catching massive swells."

The guy had bought a bodyboard instead, which was probably for the best.

Matt glanced at the clock. He needed to leave in fifteen minutes to make it to the field on time.

"Andy," he called toward the back. "You good to close tonight?"

Andy emerged from the storage room, carrying a box of new inventory. "Yeah, no problem. It's slowing down anyway."

Andy had been working at Jungle Surf for three years now, long enough that Matt trusted him completely with the evening shift. At twenty-six, he was reliable, knew the inventory as well as Matt did, and had a natural ease with customers that made him perfect for handling the dinner-hour beach crowd.

"Thanks. I owe you one."

"You owe me like fifteen at this point," Andy said with a grin, setting the box down. "But who's counting?"

Matt changed quickly in the back room, trading his Jungle Surf T-shirt and board shorts for his gray jersey and baseball pants. Andy was restocking the wetsuit display when Matt emerged in his uniform.

"You look like you're about to rob a bank," Andy said, not looking up from the rack.

"It's a baseball uniform."

"If you say so." Andy finally glanced over. "Good luck, man. Try not to blow out your shoulder on the first pitch."

"That's the spirit," Matt said dryly.

Matt grabbed his glove from under the counter and headed out onto the boardwalk. The late-afternoon crowd was thinner now, mostly families heading back from the beach, their skin pink from too much sun. The wooden boards were warm beneath his feet, and the smell of Coppertone mixed with saltwater hung in the air. Pop music drifted from one of the shops, and a kid on a bike wove past a family loaded down with chairs and boogie boards.

The drive to the field took five minutes. Matt's stomach had been doing flips since lunch, and now it felt like a knot had taken up permanent residence below his ribs. He pulled into the gravel lot to find several cars already there, teammates emerging with equipment bags and coolers.

Dan spotted him and waved. "Matt! Good to see you. Now you can meet the whole team—we only had half the guys at practice."

The introductions came fast. Braxton, the catcher he'd thrown to at practice, turned out to be a physical therapist. Kevin, first base, managed a landscaping company. Pete handled second and sold insurance. The outfielders were a mix of teachers and tradesmen. Jason and Tom were already there, chatting with a guy named Rick who apparently owned a construction company in Somers Point.

"All right, listen up!" Dan called, gathering everyone near the dugout. "We're playing against the Inlet Pirates tonight. They beat us twice last season, so let's try not to embarrass ourselves too badly."

Laughter rippled through the group.

"Matt and Austin are splitting pitching duties tonight," Dan continued. "Matt, you'll start. Austin, you'll take over around the fourth or fifth, depending on how things go."

Austin, a stocky guy in his late forties with graying temples, gave Matt a friendly nod. "No pressure, man. Just have fun with it."

Matt walked to the mound while the rest of the team took their positions. The other team was warming up in their dugout, looking just as casual and unprepared as Matt's own crew. This was beer league. Nobody was keeping stats. Nobody's career was on the line.

So why did his shoulder feel like it might seize up completely?

Braxton squatted behind home plate and gave him a simple signal—just throw it down the middle.

The first few batters came and went. Matt's pitches were all over the place—some found the strike zone, most didn't. His shoulder felt heavy after just a dozen throws, announcing its limits. But he got through it. A groundout to second, a pop fly to center, a strikeout on a batter who probably would have walked if he'd been more patient.

Then came the wild pitch.

Matt wound up and released, but the ball sailed high and inside. The batter jumped back as the ball cleared the backstop entirely, sailing into the small crowd of spectators behind the fence.

"Heads up!" someone yelled.

The ball landed directly in a guy's nachos, sending cheese

and chips flying across his lap and the woman sitting next to him.

"Are you serious right now?" the guy shouted, standing up and holding his cheese-covered hands away from his body. But he was laughing even as he said it, shaking his head in disbelief.

Matt's teammates burst out laughing. Jason doubled over in right field. Tom wasn't even pretending to hide it anymore.

"Sorry!" Matt called out, feeling his face burn.

Dan jogged over to the fence with napkins. "We'll get you another plate of nachos, man. On the house."

Matt stood on the mound, mortified, while the laughter finally died down. The next batter stepped up, clearly trying not to smile. Matt's control stayed shaky through the rest of the inning—more balls than strikes, his mechanics rusty—but by the last batter, something started to click. His release point felt more natural, and he managed to paint the corners of the strike zone twice in a row.

They made it through the first inning. Matt's shoulder felt like rubber by the time he walked back to the dugout, but they'd held the other team scoreless.

"Nice work," Austin said, clapping him on the back. "Solid first game."

Their team managed one run in the bottom of the first—a combination of walks and errors that eventually brought Tom home. Matt was grabbing his glove to head back out for the second inning when he heard a strange hissing sound.

Then water erupted from the ground.

All over the outfield, sprinkler heads popped up and began spinning, shooting water in wide arcs across the grass. Within seconds, the entire field was getting drenched.

"What in the world?" Dan yelled, already running toward the equipment shed.

Players scrambled off the field, laughing and shouting as water soaked their uniforms. Jason slipped in the grass and went down hard, sliding several feet before coming to a stop.

He lay there for a moment, then started laughing so hard he couldn't get up.

The umpire looked at the infield, already turning to mud, and threw his hands in the air. "That's it! Game's called!"

Dan emerged from the equipment shed, drenched and looking sheepish. "I forgot to change the timer! It's set for five thirty!"

"You've got to be kidding me," Kevin said, wringing water from his jersey.

"So what do we do now?" Pete asked.

"Yesterday's," Dan said immediately. "First round's on me to make up for this disaster."

The drive to Yesterday's Creekside Tavern took ten minutes, a convoy of cars heading down the island and across the 34th Street Bridge into Marmora. Matt rode with Jason and Tom, all three of them still damp and smelling vaguely of grass and dirt.

"That was the shortest game I've ever played," Tom said from the back seat.

"At least Matt got his pitching debut in before the sprinklers hit," Jason added. "How's the shoulder feeling?"

"Sore," Matt admitted. "But not terrible. I'll ice it tonight."

Yesterday's sat on Roosevelt Boulevard in Marmora, a local fixture that had been around for decades. The parking lot was already filling up with the dinner crowd, but they managed to find spots near the back. Inside, the place had that classic sports bar energy—TVs mounted everywhere showing different games, a long bar packed with people, and Eagles memorabilia covering the walls.

Dan had already claimed a section of the bar when Matt and the others arrived. Teammates were filtering in, shedding damp jerseys and ordering beers from a bartender who looked thoroughly amused by the wet baseball players invading her section.

Matt slid onto a stool between Jason and Braxton, grateful to finally sit down.

"So," Braxton said, once everyone had drinks in front of them. "That was an interesting debut."

"I destroyed someone's nachos," Matt said.

"You did," Braxton agreed cheerfully. "Guy had cheese everywhere. But hey, at least it wasn't a home run off your pitching."

Laughter erupted around the table.

"I still can't believe the sprinklers," Kevin said, shaking his head. "Dan, that was legendary incompetence."

"I know, I know," Dan said, holding up his hands. "I'll fix it before next time. I promise."

Austin, the other pitcher, leaned across the table. "Don't worry about tonight, Matt. You looked good out there before the chaos. How long's it been since you pitched?"

"Twenty years, give or take," Matt said. "Though I did throw a handful of pitches at the field the other night when we first checked it out. And I've been practicing in my backyard most days since then—just working on my delivery, trying to get my arm used to it again."

"That's smart," Austin said. "Building up slowly. How's the shoulder handling it?"

"Better than I expected, honestly. Still gets sore, but nothing like the sharp pain I used to get. I ice it after, keep the sessions short."

"Could've fooled me. Your mechanics looked solid."

"I used to play," Matt said carefully. "A long time ago."

"What level?" Rick asked. "College?"

Matt glanced at Jason, who gave him a slight nod.

"Professionally," Matt said quietly. "For the Phillies. Only for about a year and a half before I blew out my shoulder."

The bar area went silent.

"Wait," Austin said slowly. "What's your last name?"

"Woodsen," Matt said.

Austin's eyes widened. "Matt Woodsen. You're *that* Matt Woodsen?"

Matt nodded.

"You pitched for the Phillies!" Kevin said, his voice rising. "I remember watching you! You had that nasty slider!"

"I remember that too!" Pete added. "You struck out the side against the Mets that one game!"

The energy at the bar shifted completely. Everyone was leaning forward now, asking questions, recounting games they'd watched, moments they remembered.

"What happened to your shoulder?" Braxton asked, his physical therapist instincts clearly kicking in.

"Torn labrum," Matt said. "I tried to come back after surgery, but my velocity was never the same. Dropped from ninety-six to eighty-nine. In the majors, that's a death sentence for a pitcher."

"That's rough, man," Dan said. "How old were you?"

"Twenty-four when it happened. Twenty-six when I officially retired."

"And now you're back out here throwing in beer league," Austin said. "That's incredible."

"Or pathetic," Matt offered with a slight smile.

"No way," Rick said firmly. "That takes guts. Most guys would just hang up their cleats and never touch a ball again. You're still out here doing it."

The conversation gradually broadened again, but Matt noticed people kept glancing at him, like they were seeing him differently now. A few guys from other tables had overheard and came over to introduce themselves, to shake his hand, to tell him they'd watched him pitch.

"This is wild," Jason said, voice low. "You're like a celebrity here."

"I'm really not," Matt said. "I only played for about a year and a half before the injury. Most people don't even remember me."

"Doesn't matter. You played for the Phillies. In Philly, that makes you royalty."

By the time they finished dinner, Matt's shoulder was tight and throbbing, but his mood had lifted considerably. The guys on his team weren't just teammates—they were becoming friends. People who understood what it meant to love something even when you weren't great at it anymore, who showed up week after week just for the chance to play.

As they headed out to the parking lot, Dan fell into step beside Matt.

"Hey," he said. "Thanks for being cool about telling everyone your story. I know that couldn't have been easy."

"It's fine," Matt said. "It's been long enough that it doesn't hurt to talk about anymore."

"Well, we're lucky to have you. Even if you do destroy people's nachos."

Matt laughed. "I'm never going to live that down, am I?"

"Not a chance."

* * *

The old store looked different with natural light streaming through the windows.

Lauren stood back, admiring the effect of having the front windows finally unboarded. It had taken them most of the morning to pry off the plywood sheets, but now light flooded the space, illuminating dust motes that danced in the air.

"This changes everything," Claire said, cranking open one of the windows. The mechanism groaned in protest, stiff from decades of disuse. "Look at how much brighter it is."

They'd been at it since nine, armed with cleaning supplies, brooms, extra light bulbs, and a determination to see what the store could actually look like with some effort. The floors had been swept and mopped, revealing the original pine boards beneath years of grime. Half the dead bulbs had been replaced. The front door, once boarded shut, now stood propped open with a brick, letting in the ocean breeze.

Lauren dumped another dustpan full of debris into the trash bag. "I keep finding these old price tags. Look at this one—forty-five cents for a notepad."

"The prices are insane," Claire agreed. She was polishing a row of brass nautical figurines with a rag—tiny lighthouses and anchors that gleamed as the tarnish came off. "These would sell for ten, fifteen dollars each now, easy."

"So what do I call it?" Lauren asked, resting her chin on the broom handle. "If I'm actually opening this place, it needs a name."

Claire paused mid-wipe, glancing at the faded lettering above the stockroom door. "Romano's Party & Gift Shop," she read. "But that feels too formal for what this is now."

"What is it now?" Lauren asked, more to herself than to Claire.

Claire shrugged. "A vintage store? A nostalgia shop? A time capsule that happens to sell things?"

They batted around ideas while they worked. Yesteryear's. Ocean City Vintage. Nothing felt quite right.

"What about just Romano's?" Claire suggested. "Simple. Classic. It ties back to Grandma and Grandpa without being too specific."

"Romano's," Lauren repeated, testing it out. "I kind of like that. It doesn't box us into one thing."

"And it's short enough to fit on a sign."

Lauren fished her phone from her pocket to make a note, but before she could type anything, Claire's phone buzzed on the counter where she'd left it. They both glanced over to see Brian's name on the screen.

Claire's expression shuttered immediately. "I should take this."

"Do you want privacy?"

"No, it's fine." Claire answered the call, putting it on speaker. "Hey."

"Hey." Brian's voice sounded distant. "Sorry to bother you. I wanted to check in about a few things."

"Sure, what's up?"

"The mortgage company called about the Pennsylvania house. They need your signature on some refinancing paperwork so I can buy out your half of the equity. I can scan it and email it to you."

"That's fine. Just send it over."

A pause. Then: "How are you settling in? How are the kids?"

"We're good. The house is great. The kids are adjusting."

The conversation felt stilted, formal. Lauren kept sweeping, trying to give them space while still being present.

"Good, that's good," Brian said. A beat of silence. "Listen, I wanted to explain something. About the other day, when Evan called."

Claire's hands froze. "Okay."

"That was Melissa. She works in my department. We've been friends for a while, and after you left, we started spending more time together."

"I see."

"It's not what you think. Or maybe it is, I don't know. We're seeing each other now, but it didn't start until after you decided to move. I wouldn't do that to you."

The words hung in the air. Lauren watched her sister's face go rigid, her knuckles white gripping the rag.

"How long after?" Claire asked, her voice carefully neutral.

"A few weeks. Maybe a month."

"A month." Claire laughed, but there was no humor in it. "So while I was packing up our entire life, sorting through fifteen years of marriage, trying to explain to our children why their father wasn't coming with us, you were already moving on."

"Claire—"

"Was she the reason you didn't want to come? Even before the job fell through?"

"No. Of course not. The job was real, Claire. I wanted that position. But when it didn't work out..." He trailed off. "I don't know. Maybe having Melissa here made it easier to stay. Maybe I was already checked out of the marriage and didn't want to admit it. I honestly don't know."

"How long have you known her?"

"About three years. She transferred to our office in 2023."

Claire closed her eyes. "Three years."

"Nothing happened until recently. I swear."

"Do you love her?"

He took too long to answer.

"I don't know what we are yet," Brian said finally. "It's new. It's complicated."

"It's not complicated," Claire said flatly. "You chose her over your family. That's pretty straightforward."

"That's not fair."

"Isn't it?" Claire's voice rose slightly. "You had a choice. Come to Ocean City with your wife and children, start fresh, build a new life together. Or stay in Pennsylvania because a job fell through and you happened to have a convenient backup plan already waiting."

"I told you I couldn't move without a job lined up. That wasn't negotiable."

"Right. Because your job was more important than your marriage. Than your kids being near their grandparents. Than anything else."

"You're twisting this."

"I'm stating facts." Claire set down the rag, her hands shaking slightly. "You know what the worst part is? It's not even that you're seeing someone. It's that you didn't have the guts to tell me yourself. I had to find out because my son called you and she answered your phone."

"I was going to tell you."

"When? When were you going to tell me, Brian? After you proposed to her? After you moved her into our house?"

"That's not fair."

"Stop saying that's not fair!" Claire's voice rose then caught. She took a breath, steadied herself. "You don't get to lecture me about fairness. You checked out of this marriage months ago, maybe longer, and you didn't have the decency to be honest about it."

"I'm sorry," Brian said. "I handled this badly. I should have been more upfront."

"Yes, you should have."

Silence stretched between them.

"Look," Brian said. "I didn't call to fight. I just wanted you to know. I thought it would be better coming from me than from someone else."

"A little late for that."

"I know. I'm sorry."

Claire rubbed her forehead. "Is there anything else?"

"No. Just... take care of yourself, okay? And tell the kids I love them."

"I will."

She ended the call and stood there for a moment, staring at her phone. Then she set it down carefully on the counter and went back to cleaning.

"Claire," Lauren said.

"I'm fine."

"You're not fine."

"I told myself I wasn't going to do that," Claire said. "I was going to stay calm, not ask questions, not dig into it. And then he started talking, and I just..." She shook her head.

Claire scrubbed at the shelf, her movements methodical. "I knew there had to be someone. You don't just give up on fifteen years of marriage because a job falls through. There had to be a reason he was so quick to let me go." She sounded matter-of-fact, almost detached. "I've been telling myself it didn't matter, that I didn't need to know. But hearing it confirmed..." She stopped, examining the shelf she'd been cleaning. "Three years. He knew her for three years."

Lauren set her broom aside. "Do you think it was going on the whole time?"

"I don't know. Maybe. Maybe not." Claire kept working, wiping in small, careful circles. "I keep thinking about all those late nights at work, all the times he said he was too tired to talk about anything real. Was it her? Or was it just us falling apart and I didn't want to see it?"

"You trusted him."

"I did." Claire paused. "I really thought—even after he said he wasn't coming, even after we signed the papers—part of me kept thinking maybe he'd change his mind. Show up one day with his car packed, ready to try again." She let out a short laugh. "Stupid, right?"

"Not stupid. Hopeful."

"Same thing, apparently." Claire dropped the rag in the bucket. "I pushed for this move. I fell in love with this house before we even had a plan. Maybe if I'd been more cautious, more practical—"

"Stop," Lauren said firmly. "Don't do that. Don't take responsibility for his choices."

Claire was quiet for a long moment, staring at the dust-covered shelves. When she spoke again, her tone was softer, more contemplative. "It's strange. I've been so busy—packing, moving, settling the kids, opening this store. I haven't had time to really feel it, you know? But now..." She picked up the rag again. "Now it's real. He's with someone else. He's building a life without us. And I'm standing in my grandparents' abandoned store, covered in dust, trying to figure out who I am without him."

"You're still you."

"Am I?" Claire turned to look at Lauren. "I've been Brian's

wife for fifteen years. Before that I was Brian's girlfriend. I don't know who I am separate from that. I don't know what I want or who I want to be. I just know I'm here, and he's there, and somehow I have to figure out the rest."

"You will."

"Maybe." Claire turned back to the shelves, her movements purposeful again. "But right now, I need to keep working. If I stop moving, I'll start thinking too much."

They worked in silence for a while, the only sounds the soft swish of the broom and the occasional car passing outside. The store was taking shape around them, slowly revealing itself as something that could actually function again.

"What do you think?" Claire asked eventually, surveying their progress. "Can we really open this place?"

Lauren looked around. The main floor was mostly clean now, the windows shining, the shelves organized into some semblance of order. They still had pricing to figure out, signage to create, a dozen other details to handle. But it was possible.

"Yeah," she said. "I think we can."

Claire nodded slowly. "Romano's."

"Romano's," Lauren agreed.

They spent another hour cleaning, their earlier conversation settling into something they'd have to revisit later. But for now, there was work to do.

CHAPTER NINE

Bay Avenue stretched ahead in the midmorning sun, the marsh on one side sending up its familiar smell of salt and mud. Brenna stood at the roadside in her orange safety vest, facing the small group of volunteers she'd assembled for training. Seven people had shown up—more than she'd expected when she'd put the call out on social media three days ago.

"The key is to watch where the marsh meets the road," Brenna explained, gesturing toward the green expanse beside them. "Terrapins are most active from mid-morning through early afternoon during nesting season, when the sun warms them up. Females will emerge from the marsh and attempt to cross to reach suitable nesting sites—sandy, sunny areas above the high tide line like road shoulders, disturbed soil near the marsh edge, anywhere with sun and well-drained sand." She held up a laminated card with photos. "Look for the dark spots and markings on the light-gray skin, the diamond-patterned shell. They move slowly, so they're extremely vulnerable to vehicles."

Adrienne, the woman in her seventies who'd been the first to volunteer, nodded along. Two college students from

Stockton were taking notes. A middle-aged man named Robert who'd found a dead terrapin in his driveway last week stood with his arms crossed, listening intently. Three others—a retired couple and a young woman who worked remotely—had driven from nearby Somers Point specifically to help.

"When you spot one crossing, your job is simple," Brenna continued. "Put on your vest, use the portable traffic cones to slow approaching vehicles, and carefully pick up the turtle and carry it across to the side it was heading toward. Never turn a turtle around—they're determined to reach their nesting site, and they'll just try to cross again."

"What if someone won't stop?" one of the college students asked.

"Most people will slow down if they see you. But safety first —yours and the turtle's. If traffic won't cooperate, document the location and time, and we'll add it to our data on high-risk areas."

A pickup truck slowed as it passed, the driver leaning out the window. "What're you all looking for out here?"

"Terrapins," Brenna called back. "We're training volunteers to help them cross safely during nesting season."

"No kidding. Good luck with it!" He drove on.

She turned back to the volunteers, feeling a small surge of optimism.

"Let's walk down into the marsh," Brenna said. "I want to show you what we're protecting here—it's not just about the terrapins."

They followed her down a narrow path through the cord-grass, the ground spongy beneath their feet. The tide was coming in, water trickling through the network of tidal creeks that crisscrossed the marsh.

"This ecosystem is one of the most productive on the planet," Brenna explained. "Salt marshes like this one provide critical nursery habitat for most of the fish and shellfish we catch commercially—striped bass, flounder, blue crabs, shrimp. They filter pollutants from runoff before it reaches the bay. They protect against storm surge during hurricanes. And they're home to specially adapted species found only in brackish coastal habitats."

She pointed to a cluster of small snails clinging to a stem of cordgrass. "Marsh snails—one of the terrapins' main food sources. And look there."

A snowy egret stood motionless in a shallow pool, neck extended, waiting for fish. As they watched, it struck with lightning speed, coming up with a killifish in its beak. The bird tilted its head back and swallowed, then resumed its patient watch.

"How many terrapins are we talking about?" Robert asked. "In this marsh, I mean."

"Based on our surveys this season, we've documented approximately two hundred individuals in the marsh systems around Corson's Inlet and the northern bay areas. That might sound like a lot, but when you factor in road mortality during nesting season..." She paused, watching a marsh wren dart through the reeds. "We've already lost twenty females since May first. Each one of those could have laid multiple clutches, eight to twelve eggs per clutch."

"That's devastating," the young woman from Somers Point said quietly.

"Exactly. But that's why we're here. That's why this matters."

Movement in the water caught Brenna's eye—something larger than a killifish, something that didn't belong. She squinted against the sun, then her expression shifted.

"Stay here," she said to the volunteers, her tone changing. "I need to check something."

She walked along the creek bank, following the movement. A kayak came into view, tucked into a narrow channel where the cordgrass grew thick. A man in waders stood in the shallow water, and Brenna could see what he was doing—pulling gill nets from the creek, checking them for fish.

"Excuse me," she called out.

The man looked up, startled. He was maybe forty, baseball cap pulled low, hands full of netting.

"Are you aware this area is closed to gill netting during spawning season?" Brenna asked, keeping her voice even. "May through July."

"I didn't see any signs," he said, though he didn't sound convincing.

"There are signs posted at both channel entrances. Gill nets can trap terrapins and other wildlife—they get tangled and drown."

The man let out an exasperated breath. "You're going to make a big deal out of a few fish?"

"I'm asking you to follow the regulations that protect the spawning grounds."

They stared at each other for a long moment. Then the man muttered something under his breath and started gathering his nets, hauling them into his kayak.

Brenna watched as he paddled away, his kayak cutting through the narrow channel until it disappeared around a bend in the marsh.

She walked back to where her volunteers waited, all of them watching with wide eyes.

"Does that happen often?" the other Stockton student asked.

"More than it should. People think because the marsh isn't obviously patrolled, they can do whatever they want. But there are regulations for a reason." She gestured out at the wetlands around them. "The marsh might look like empty wilderness, but it's critical habitat. Everything here is connected."

They spent another thirty minutes exploring, Brenna pointing out blue crabs moving sideways through the shallows and explaining how the marsh provided shelter for juvenile crabs before they moved into deeper water. She talked about the tidal cycles, how the marsh flooded twice daily with nutrient-rich water that fed the entire ecosystem.

By the time they walked back to Bay Avenue, the sun was approaching its midday height, and sounds filled the marsh—bird calls, the rustle of wind through the grass.

"We'll start actual monitoring shifts tomorrow," Brenna said. "I'll text everyone the schedule tonight. We'll focus on midmorning through early afternoon first—that's when females are most actively crossing."

"I can take a couple weekday mornings," Adrienne offered. "I'm retired. Might as well put the time to good use."

"I've got weekends," Robert said.

The others said they'd check their schedules and get back to her. Brenna nodded, doing the math in her head. Seven volunteers, maybe ten hours of coverage a week between them —if everyone followed through. Bay Avenue alone needed more than that. It wasn't nearly enough—but it was more than she'd had last week.

As the volunteers dispersed to their cars, Brenna stood alone on Bay Avenue, looking out at the marsh. The tide was still coming in, carrying life into the system. Somewhere in there, terrapins were going about their ancient rhythms, unaware that people were finally trying to help them survive in a changing landscape.

Her phone rang—a number she recognized. The animal hospital.

"Hi, it's Josh. Dr. Grant." His voice was professional but friendly. "I wanted to give you an update on your terrapin patient."

"How is she doing?"

"Really well, actually. She's eating, moving around her recovery tank. The epoxy repair is holding perfectly, and there's no sign of infection. I'm impressed with how resilient these guys are."

"That's great news. When do you think she'll be ready for transfer to the research center?"

"At the rate she's healing? Maybe a couple days. I was thinking you could pick her up later this week if that works for you." He paused. "How's the protection campaign going?"

Brenna leaned against her truck. "I just finished training volunteers for road monitoring—had seven people show up this morning. Even had to chase off a guy gill netting illegally in the spawning grounds, but other than that, it went well."

Josh laughed. "Of course you did. So let me get this straight—you're training volunteers, chasing off rule-breakers, and somehow still finding time to answer on the first ring?"

"I wasn't waiting by the phone," Brenna said, though she absolutely had answered quickly.

"Sure you weren't." His tone was light, teasing. "For the record, I'm impressed. Not everyone takes on the entire fishing community before lunch."

"It was one guy with a net."

"Still counts." She could hear the smile in his voice. "So what's the long-term goal? Besides confronting fishermen and training an army of turtle rescuers?"

Brenna laughed. "Ideally, we monitor, collect data, show a measurable decrease in road mortality by end of season. Long-term is getting permanent protections in place, but that's years away."

"Sounds like you're in this for the long haul."

"Someone has to be."

"I admire that," he said, his voice dropping slightly. "People who care about things enough to actually do something about them."

A flutter of warmth spread through Brenna's chest. "Well, it helps when people like you patch them up after they get hit."

"Just doing my job," he said, though something in his tone suggested it was more than that. "Though I have to say, this is the most interesting case I've had in a while. Getting to use wildlife medicine skills again—it reminded me why I love the work."

"I thought you said wildlife medicine was why you became a vet?"

"It was. Is. I don't get to use those skills as often as I'd like in a general practice." He paused. "So thanks for that."

"I think you did the hard part."

"We make a good team, then."

The words hung in the air. Brenna found herself smiling, her cheeks flushing in a way that had nothing to do with the midday sun.

"I should let you get back to work," she said finally.

"Yeah. I'll give you a call when she's ready for pickup."

"Sounds good."

"Talk soon, Brenna."

She ended the call and stood there for a moment, still smiling, before heading back to her truck.

* * *

Claire wandered from room to room, straightening pillows that didn't need straightening, closing drawers that were already closed. She'd dropped the kids off at tennis lessons ten minutes ago—Bridget excited, Evan dragging his feet but going anyway. Without them, the house felt like it was holding its breath.

She'd been awake since six, unable to fall back asleep, her mind churning through the conversation with Brian. Melissa. The woman had a name now, which somehow made it worse. Before, she'd been abstract—a possibility, a fear that Claire could push aside. Now she was real. Someone Brian had known for three years, someone who worked in his department, someone in his life while Claire unpacked boxes in Ocean City.

She made her way to the sunroom, settling into the spot on the couch that had become hers over the past week. Through the windows, she could see a woman walking two dogs, a delivery truck making its morning rounds.

She should be doing something productive. There were still a few pictures that needed hanging, the kids' rooms waiting for curtains, the overgrown backyard calling for attention. She should be working—her laptop sat on the coffee table, emails probably piling up. But she couldn't summon the energy for any of it.

She found herself remembering.

Six years ago, she and Brian had come to Ocean City for a long weekend. It was July, peak summer season, and they'd rented an apartment just off the beach. They'd developed a morning routine during that trip—walk to Ove's for donuts and coffee, then find a spot on the boardwalk to eat while people-watching. It had felt perfect then, like a glimpse of what their life could be if they ever made the move permanent.

Claire grabbed her keys. Instead of staying in the empty house, she walked toward the boardwalk.

The streets were calm, most of the early-season visitors still waking up. Claire walked slowly, breathing in the salt air, feeling the breeze off the ocean. The boardwalk stretched ahead, not yet crowded with the afternoon beach rush.

Through Ove's window, Claire could see people sitting at tables eating breakfast, the smell of fresh-made donuts drifting out. She stopped at the takeout window, suddenly uncertain.

They'd always gotten the same order. Black coffee for Brian, black coffee for her. Cinnamon sugar apple cider donuts to share. They'd find their usual spot, sit close together, plan their day while finishing breakfast.

A young woman at the window smiled at her. "What can I get you?"

"Coffee and a honey-glazed donut, please."

Claire paid and carried her order down the boardwalk, the coffee cup solid and real in her hands. She passed the bench she and Brian used to claim. An older couple sat there now, holding hands, watching the world go by.

Claire kept walking.

She found an empty bench farther down. The dunes blocked the view of the water, but she could hear the waves. People walked past—families with strollers, a group of teenagers laughing.

Claire sat, balancing the coffee and donut bag on her lap. The bench was slightly weathered, the wood worn smooth by years of people sitting in this exact spot. How many of them had been alone? How many had been processing loss or change or the terrifying freedom of starting over?

She took a sip of the coffee. Strong, hot, simple. She took another sip then pulled out the honey-glazed donut.

It was still warm, the honey glaze sweet and sticky on her fingers. She and Brian had always gotten cinnamon sugar—it was what you got at Ove's, he'd said, like it was a rule. Today she'd wanted something different. She bit into it without hesitation.

The honey was sweeter than she expected, richer than the familiar cinnamon sugar. Different. Good different.

She sat there, eating her donut and drinking her coffee, watching people pass by. A couple her age strolled by, the man's arm around the woman's shoulders, both of them laughing. Claire felt a pang—not of jealousy exactly, but of loss. That had been her and Brian once. When had they stopped laughing like that?

But as she watched them disappear, the pang shifted. Lifted. Because sitting here alone, doing this just for herself on a random morning—she felt something she hadn't expected.

She felt okay.

Not happy, not yet. But steady. Like maybe this wasn't the end of her story but the beginning of a new chapter. One where she got to choose the donut and the bench. Where she could walk the boardwalk alone without feeling like something was missing.

She stood, threw away her trash, and started walking back toward the house. Not rushing, just walking. Taking her time.

On impulse, she turned down a side street she'd never explored before, one lined with little cottages painted in pastels. Gardens overflowed with beach roses and irises. A cat watched her from a porch railing. An older man watering his plants waved, and she waved back.

She continued on, no destination in mind, just following wherever the streets led her. On the next block, she passed a yoga studio tucked between two houses, its windows open to the morning air. A handwritten sign advertised drop-in classes. Claire paused, watching a few women inside moving through poses. She'd always wanted to try yoga but never had. She pulled out her phone and took a photo of the schedule.

A few blocks farther, she discovered a shop that was new to her—a tiny storefront with a hand-painted sign that read "Salt & Story." The window display was a jumble of things that made her heart rise: journals with cloth covers, beeswax candles, vintage postcards, stacks of paperback novels. A basket of bright stickers sat next to a ceramic bowl filled with sea glass.

Claire pushed open the door. A bell chimed overhead, and the smell of lavender and old paper wrapped around her. She wandered the narrow aisles, running her fingers over the textured bindings, reading the titles on book spines. There was no rush. No one waiting for her. No one asking when she'd be done.

She left twenty minutes later with a small paper bag: a journal with a blue linen cover, a candle that smelled like the ocean, and a sheet of stickers covered in tiny illustrations of shells and starfish. Silly, maybe. But hers.

This could be her life now. Walking streets she'd never walked, finding studios where she might learn something new,

discovering shops full of unexpected treasures. Building something new from the pieces of what had broken.

By the time she reached home, the house didn't feel quite
as empty. She set her bag on the kitchen counter and smiled at
the purchases inside. She had fifteen minutes before she needed
to pick up the kids from tennis. Just enough time to flip through
that journal, start thinking about what she wanted to fill it with.

CHAPTER TEN

Maddie stood on solid ground, her feet planted on the boardwalk instead of the lift platform. The upper sections of the mural were finished now—the sky gradient complete, the wave's crest restored and better than before. No trace of the red spray paint remained; she'd buried it under fresh layers of blue and white, reclaiming every inch. What remained was the bottom third, the portion she could reach from a stepladder. The foam pattern where the wave met the boardwalk. The final details that would tie everything together. Another day of work, and it would be done.

She'd been dreading this part, actually. Up on the lift, she'd had distance from the crowds, a buffer of height between herself and the constant flow of locals and tourists. Down here, people stopped to watch. They hovered. They asked questions. They offered opinions she hadn't requested.

But she'd come this far, and that knowledge kept her going.

Two small cameras mounted on the arcade's corner watched over everything. Steve had installed them the day after the vandalism, a constant reminder that someone was paying attention now. The boardwalk businesses had all promised to keep an eye out too. The bookstore owner. The guy who ran the T-shirt shop. Even the salt water taffy store owner had stopped by twice to check on her progress.

Maddie loaded her brush with titanium white and began working on the foam, building up texture with short, deliberate strokes. The May morning was already humid and close, the kind of weather that made her clothes stick to her skin. She'd pulled her hair into a bun to keep it off her neck, but stray pieces kept escaping, plastering themselves to her forehead.

She'd been at it since six, taking only a short break for water and a granola bar. Part of her wanted to draw it out, to stay in this creative space a little longer. But a bigger part wanted to see it done. Complete. Protected in a way the vandalism had proven it wasn't.

By midmorning, her back ached from bending and her arms felt heavy. She'd gone through two water bottles and reapplied sunscreen three times. The humidity had turned oppressive, making every breath feel like work. She needed a break. A real one.

She was cleaning her brushes when she heard footsteps behind her.

"You look like you need to cool off," Dominic said.

She turned to find him holding two cold bottles of fizzy mineral water, his dark hair escaping from beneath a backward cap. He wore board shorts and a faded T-shirt, the casual uniform of a day off.

"You have no idea," Maddie said, accepting one of the bottles and pressing it against her forehead. "I think I sweated through everything I'm wearing."

"I'm not complaining."

"You're biased."

Dominic grinned. "So here's a thought. OC Waterpark is right there." He gestured toward the water park, visible just down the boardwalk, its slides and attractions catching the late morning light. "It's hot. You're hot. Not in the good way, although also in the good way. Why don't we take a break?"

"I should probably keep working. I want to finish before—"

"The mural will still be there tomorrow," Dominic interrupted. "You've been out here painting for four hours. Even I take breaks."

Maddie laughed. "Debatable."

"The point stands. Come on. An hour or two. Cool off, have some fun. When's the last time you did something just for fun?"

She tried to remember. The gallery kept her busy. The mural had consumed everything else. Before that, winter had been slow and quiet, and before that...

"See?" Dominic said, reading her expression. "Too long. Let's go."

"I don't have a bathing suit."

"There's a shop two blocks from here. They sell swimsuits for like fifteen bucks. Problem solved."

Maddie hesitated, looking up at the mural. The cameras blinked their red lights. The wave gleamed in the morning sun, waiting for her return.

"One hour," she said finally. "Maybe two."

"That's the spirit."

* * *

The water park sat right on the boardwalk, a compact collection of slides, pools, and a lazy river that drew steady crowds all summer. Dominic had somehow talked the attendant into giving them access to a cabana, which turned out to be a shaded platform with lounge chairs and a small table.

Maddie emerged from the bathroom in her new purchase: a simple navy-blue one-piece that had been on sale. Nothing fancy, but it fit well enough, and her painting clothes were soaked anyway.

Dominic was waiting by the cabana, and when he saw her,

something shifted in his expression. Not obvious, just a slight widening of his eyes, a softening around his mouth.

"What?" Maddie asked, suddenly self-conscious.

"Nothing. Just—you look good."

"I look like a woman who's been painting since six in the morning."

"You look good," he repeated, and the sincerity in his voice made her cheeks flush.

They started with the lazy river, floating on tubes through the winding channel. The water was cool but not cold, and Maddie felt the tension in her shoulders begin to melt. Kids paddled past them, shrieking with joy. A family bobbed in a cluster nearby, the parents looking exhausted but happy.

The current carried them around a bend, and Maddie closed her eyes, letting herself drift. The sounds of the crowd faded, replaced by splashing water and laughter.

"This was a good idea," she admitted, tilting her head back.

"I'm full of good ideas."

"Let's not get carried away."

Dominic laughed, reaching over to splash water at her. She splashed back, and for a few minutes they were just two people being silly in a lazy river, the stress of vandalism and repairs and deadlines washing away.

A lifeguard on duty gave them a half-hearted warning about roughhousing, but he was smiling. Mid-May meant the summer rules weren't being strictly enforced yet. The park had the relaxed energy of a place still warming up for its busy season.

They went around twice then a third time, neither of them in any hurry. Maddie found herself thinking about her mural differently. Not as a project to finish, but as something that existed in the world. Something people could see and respond to. The vandalism had felt like a violation, but maybe it had also been a twisted kind of compliment. Someone had noticed her work enough to want to destroy it.

She was still mulling that over when she spotted the slides.

"Those," she said, pointing to the towering slides that twisted down from a platform high above the park. "I want to go on those."

"The big ones?" Dominic raised an eyebrow. "Those are intense."

"I spent weeks on a lift eighteen feet in the air. I think I can handle a water slide."

The climb to the top took longer than expected. Stairs wound around the tower in a seemingly endless spiral, and by the time they reached the platform, Maddie was slightly winded but exhilarated. Other people waited in line ahead of them, a mix of teenagers and a few brave parents. The sound of rushing water filled the air, punctuated by distant screams of delight.

But it was the view that stopped Maddie in her tracks.

The entire boardwalk stretched out before them, a ribbon of activity and color running parallel to the beach. She could see the Ferris wheel at Playland's Castaway Cove, the colorful umbrellas dotting the sand, the ocean sparkling beyond the dunes. The salt breeze reached even up here, carrying with it the familiar scents of summer—sunscreen and french fries and something floral from one of the boardwalk shops.

And there, visible from this height, was her mural.

Maddie's breath caught. She'd never seen it from this angle before, from this distance. The wave looked different from up here. More dynamic somehow, more alive. The colors she'd agonized over blended together into something cohesive and whole.

"Oh wow," said a woman behind her, following Maddie's gaze. "Is that new? That mural on the arcade?"

"I noticed it yesterday," her companion said. "It's gorgeous. Whoever painted that really knows what they're doing."

"It's incredible," the first woman continued. "The colors are so vivid. My kids love it. They make me walk past it every time we go to the beach."

"It really captures the feeling of being at the shore," the second woman added. "You know? That moment right before a wave crashes. I don't know who painted it, but they should be proud."

Dominic caught Maddie's eye and smiled. She felt her throat tighten, but in a good way. They stood there together, listening as the women continued to discuss the mural, pointing out details, debating whether the wave was meant to be crashing or curling. Neither Maddie nor Dominic said a word. They didn't need to.

The women eventually headed toward the slide, still chatting about the boardwalk and their plans for the day. Maddie pulled him toward the slide entrance.

The slide was everything she needed. Speed and water and pure, unthinking joy as she raced down the twisting turns, the world reduced to motion and sensation. She hit the pool at the bottom laughing, Dominic landing seconds later.

They went again. And again. Like kids, she thought. Like happy, carefree kids who had nothing to worry about except which one to try next.

They spent another hour in the park, alternating between slides and the lazy river, occasionally retreating to their cabana for water and rest. By the time they left, it was early afternoon, and Maddie felt lighter than she had in weeks. One more day of touch-ups and the mural would be complete—her work on permanent display for thousands of beachgoers to see every summer.

* * *

Nancy and Joe stopped at the Welcome Center on their way back from Somers Point, a routine that had become almost automatic over the past week. They each had their own binoculars now. Joe had his out before Nancy even turned off the ignition. The weather was perfect for viewing—clear sky, light breeze, good visibility across the marsh.

They headed to the railing first, checking the rookery. The white egrets and herons were active in the trees, tending their nests as usual. Everything looked normal.

"I heard you can walk under the bridge to get a closer look," Nancy said. "Want to try it?"

"Sure."

The path wound beneath the bridge, descending toward the water level, where serious birders often gathered. Sure enough, a cluster of people had set up on one side of the path—folding stools, massive telephoto lenses on tripods, the unmistakable posture of people waiting for the perfect shot. They were all aimed toward the rookery, toward the nest colonies Nancy and Joe had been watching all week.

Nancy raised her binoculars to scan the marsh beyond the trees, where patches of shallow water and grass were now visible from this lower angle. That was when she saw it. A flash of pink among the green. A color that didn't belong.

"Joe." She kept her voice low. "You need to see this."

He raised his binoculars quickly. She heard his sharp intake of breath.

"What is that?"

Nancy refocused, turning the focus wheel until the image sharpened. Her heart began to pound.

It was large, wading in a patch of marsh about fifty yards out. Long legs, curved neck. And the color—a soft coral pink that seemed almost unreal against the green marsh grass. Its bill was the strangest thing, flat and wide, shaped like a serving spoon.

"I have no idea," Nancy whispered. "But look at that bill."

She dropped the binoculars to her chest and rifled through her bag for the field guide they'd been carrying everywhere.

She flipped through the pages, hands trembling slightly, scanning the waterbirds section. There—pink plumage, that distinctive spatulate bill.

"It's a spoonbill," she said, her voice tight with excitement. "A roseate spoonbill. See here. Roseate spoonbill. Range: coastal southeastern United States, mainly Florida and Texas."

"Florida and Texas?" Joe said. "What's it doing here?"

"It's listed as a rare vagrant to the mid-Atlantic," Nancy read. "That means it's not supposed to be here. Sometimes birds wander outside their normal range, especially after breeding season or during migration." She looked up at Joe, her pulse quickening. "This is rare. Really rare."

Joe was already moving along the path to get a better view. "Come on. Let's get closer."

None of the photographers seemed to have noticed the spoonbill.

"Other side," Nancy murmured to Joe, steering him away from the crowd. "The bird's over there."

They made their way quietly along the path until they reached a spot with a clear view. The spoonbill was still there, still real, its pink feathers glowing against the morning light. It swept its bill through the shallow water in slow, methodical arcs, feeding.

"Well, I'll be."

Nancy turned to find an older man settling onto a folding stool beside them. He was dressed head to toe in camouflage, including a hat with a mesh face covering pushed up on top of his head. His binoculars looked like they cost more than Nancy's car. A well-worn canvas bag at his feet bulged with what appeared to be field guides, snacks, and more optical equipment.

"You see it too?" Nancy asked.

"Been watching her for twenty minutes." The man's voice was a low rasp, like gravel in a blender. "Name's Earl. Been birding these marshes for forty years. Never seen one of these up here."

"We're Nancy and Joe," Nancy said. "We just started birding about a week ago."

Earl let out a bark of laughter that startled a sparrow from a nearby bush. "Just started, and you're spotting roseate spoonbills? That's some beginner's luck. Most folks bird for decades before they stumble onto something this good." He shook his head, grinning beneath a bushy gray mustache. "Those folks over there"—he jerked his thumb toward the photographers —"they've been here since dawn, waiting for the egrets to do something interesting. Haven't looked left once. Too busy comparing their lens sizes."

"Should we tell them?" Joe asked.

"And ruin my peace and quiet? No, thank you." Earl adjusted his binoculars then pulled a small notebook from his pocket and jotted something down. "They'll figure it out eventually. Or they won't. Either way, we get to enjoy the show."

Nancy turned back to the spoonbill. It was still feeding, that distinctive sweeping motion mesmerizing to watch. The bird moved with a kind of prehistoric grace, its flat bill cutting through the water like a paddle. She opened the field guide again, reading aloud in a whisper.

"'Roseate spoonbills feed by touch, swinging their bills through the water to detect prey. Diet includes small fish, aquatic invertebrates, and crustaceans. The pink coloration comes from carotenoid pigments in their food.'"

"So they're pink because of what they eat?" Joe said.

"Like flamingos," Earl confirmed. "This one's probably a juvenile or young adult—see how the pink isn't as intense? The older they get, the brighter they turn. Give her a few years and she'll be hot pink."

"What's she doing up here?" Nancy wondered.

"Post-breeding dispersal, most likely. After nesting season, some birds wander north looking for new territory. We're also seeing more southern species push north as things warm up—the bay's a few degrees warmer than it used to be, and that means more food for birds like her. Usually doesn't happen until late summer, so she's early. Or she's an adventurer." Earl chuckled. "I like to think she just wanted to see what all the fuss was about."

They watched in companionable silence as the spoonbill continued feeding. Occasionally it would pause, survey its surroundings, then return to its steady rhythm. A great egret landed nearby and seemed startled by the pink intruder, giving it a wide berth before settling down to its own fishing.

"How long have you been birding?" Joe wondered aloud.

"Most of my life, I reckon. Started with my grandfather—he had a farm in Millville, and we'd go out at dawn to watch the hawks come off the ridge during fall migration. Got hooked." Earl lowered his binoculars and fixed them with a shrewd look. "You two picked a good spot to start. This marsh is special. More bird species come through here than most people realize. You just have to know where to look. And when to keep your mouth shut."

"We found the rookery by accident," Nancy admitted. "Stopped to use the bathroom and ended up watching the ibis nest for an hour."

Earl let out another gravelly laugh. "Best discoveries are always by accident. That's how I found my first snowy owl—got lost driving home from a funeral down at Cape May, pulled over to figure out where I was, and there she was. Sitting on a fence post like she'd been waiting for me. Stayed for twenty minutes, just the two of us. Changed my whole life." He scratched at his mustache. "Course, these days everybody's got to post everything online the second they see it. Ruins the magic, if you ask me. Some things should stay between you and the bird."

"Do you think the spoonbill will stay?" Joe's voice broke the silence.

"Hard to say. Sometimes they pass through in a day or two. Sometimes they stick around all summer if the feeding's good." Earl shrugged. "Best thing is to enjoy it while it's here. That's the secret to birding. Maybe to everything."

The spoonbill raised its head just then, as if aware of their admiration. The late morning sun illuminated its coral plumage, every feather vivid and clear.

"Would you look at that," Earl murmured. "Forty years, and the birds can still surprise me."

A commotion from the photographers' side of the path interrupted them. One of them had finally noticed, pointing excitedly, and suddenly the whole group was in motion—tripods being repositioned, telephoto lenses swinging around, voices rising.

"Well," Earl sighed, "there goes the neighborhood."

The photographers descended on their section of the path, a chaos of equipment and exclamations. Nancy and Joe stepped back to make room as at least eight people crowded in, jostling for position, cameras clicking furiously.

"Roseate spoonbill! Here in Ocean City!"

"Did you get the shot?"

"Move your tripod, you're in my frame!"

"I can't believe it—I've never seen one in New Jersey!"

The spoonbill, understandably startled by the sudden attention, lifted its head. It regarded the crowd with what Nancy could have sworn was disdain, then spread its wings—displaying the full glory of its pink plumage—and took off, heading south along the marsh.

"No! Come back!"

"Did anyone get the flight shot?"

The photographers scrambled to track its departure, but the bird was already disappearing behind the tree line, a flash of pink swallowed by green.

Earl shook his head, but he was smiling. "Every time. Every

single time. They scare off the bird with all that racket, then wonder why it left."

Nancy felt a pang of disappointment, but it faded quickly. She'd seen it. Really seen it. That extraordinary pink bird, feeding in the marsh like it belonged here, like it was the most natural thing in the world.

"Thank you," she said to Earl. "For sharing this with us."

"Nothing to share. We were all just watching the same bird." But Earl looked pleased. "You come back tomorrow morning, around seven. Chances are she'll return to feed. Birds are creatures of habit."

"We will," Joe said.

They walked back up the path, leaving the photographers to argue about whose fault it was the bird had flown. Nancy held the field guide close to her chest, already planning to look up more about roseate spoonbills when they got home.

"That was incredible," she said to Joe as they reached the car.

"Best day of birding yet," he agreed. "And we've only been at this for a week."

Nancy looked back toward the marsh, toward the rookery still teeming with white birds, toward the spot where a pink visitor had graced them with her presence.

"Earl was right," she said. "Enjoy it while it's here. That's the secret."

CHAPTER ELEVEN

Brenna pulled her truck onto the gravel shoulder of Bay Avenue, parking behind the news van that had arrived a few minutes earlier. She grabbed her orange safety vest from the passenger seat and stepped out into the morning air, thick with salt and the familiar brackish smell of the marsh.

The cameraman, a stocky guy named Larry, was already unloading equipment from the van's back doors. "We'll set up here," he called to her. "The marsh is visible in the background, and we can get the road in the shot. Perfect visual for explaining the crossing problem."

The reporter, a woman in her early thirties named Paula Drew, was touching up her makeup using the van's side mirror. She'd called Brenna yesterday to go over the segment, asking pointed questions about terrapin biology and the scope of the problem. Now came the live portion.

"Two minutes," Larry called, adjusting his camera on its tripod.

Brenna's pulse kicked up a notch. She'd given presentations to township councils, spoken at academic conferences, led volunteer training sessions. But live television was different. No second takes. No editing out the awkward pauses.

"Nervous?" Paula asked, tucking a strand of dark hair behind her ear.

"A little."

"Don't be. Just talk to me like we're having a conversation. Pretend the camera isn't there."

Easy for her to say.

A car passed, slowing as the driver craned to see what was happening. That was the whole point of this segment. Get people's attention. Make them care.

"Thirty seconds," Larry said.

Paula positioned herself beside Brenna, angling so the marsh and road were both visible behind them. The wind picked up slightly, ruffling the cordgrass in the distance. A great egret lifted from the shallows, its white wings catching the light as it glided toward a tidal creek.

"And we're live in five, four, three..."

The red light on the camera blinked on.

"Good morning! I'm Paula Drew, reporting live from Bay Avenue in Ocean City, where a coastal ecologist is working to protect one of New Jersey's most unique species." Paula turned slightly toward Brenna. "I'm here with Brenna Groff from the coastal research center. Brenna, tell us what's happening here."

Brenna took a breath. "Every spring, female diamondback terrapins leave the safety of the salt marsh to find nesting sites on higher ground. They have to lay their eggs above the high tide line, or the nests will flood and the eggs won't survive. The problem is, to reach those sites, they have to cross roads like this one." She gestured toward the asphalt. "And every year, dozens of females are killed by vehicles."

"How significant is this problem?"

"We've documented over thirty road-killed terrapins in this area since May first alone. Each of those was likely a breeding female, carrying eight to twelve eggs. When you do the math, that's potentially hundreds of baby turtles that will never hatch."

Paula's expression shifted to genuine concern. "That's devastating. What's being done about it?"

"We've launched a volunteer monitoring program. Right now, we have a small but dedicated group patrolling high-risk road crossings during peak nesting hours, helping turtles cross safely. But we need more help." Brenna looked directly at the camera, channeling every ounce of passion she felt for this work. "If anyone watching wants to make a real difference for local wildlife, we're looking for volunteers. You don't need any special training. Just a willingness to show up."

"Has the program made a difference so far?"

"It has. Since we started, we've helped fifty-three terrapins cross safely. We've rescued six injured females and successfully incubated nineteen eggs from turtles that didn't make it. Those hatchlings will be released into the marsh this fall." Brenna paused, letting that sink in. "It takes a community. We've got retirees spending their mornings on patrol, college students doing monitoring shifts between classes, families who come out together on weekends. The township has agreed to install additional warning signage along the worst stretches of road, and we're in preliminary talks about wildlife underpasses for next year."

"How can people get involved?"

"They can email me through the research center or message us on Facebook. We'll get them trained and assigned to a shift within a week."

Larry gave a subtle signal, and Paula wrapped up the segment with contact information scrolling across the bottom of the screen. The red light blinked off.

"That was great," Paula said, enthusiasm in her voice. "You're a natural."

Brenna laughed, tension releasing from her shoulders. "I didn't stumble over anything?"

"Not once. And the background was perfect. Did you see

that egret fly past right as we started? Couldn't have planned it better."

They filmed a few more shots for the evening broadcast: B-roll of the marsh, the road, the faded turtle crossing sign. Brenna pointed out where volunteers had been stationed yesterday, described what a successful rescue looked like.

By the time the news van pulled away, it was nearly ten o'clock. Brenna checked her phone and found it buzzing with notifications. Her breath caught as she scrolled through them.

Eighteen new Facebook messages. Twelve emails through the research center's contact form.

The first message was from a woman in Marmora: "Saw your segment this morning. I work from home and can volunteer weekday mornings. Please let me know how to sign up."

The second was from a retired teacher in Somers Point who'd been a birder for decades but never knew about the terrapins.

The third was from a family with teenagers who wanted to help as a summer project.

She kept scrolling, each message a small affirmation that the segment had worked. People had seen it. People cared.

Her phone buzzed again. A text from Josh: "Good news—the turtle's ready for pickup today if you have time."

Martha. That was what Brenna had started calling the turtle in her head. Giving her a name probably meant she was getting too attached, but she didn't care.

She typed back: "I can come today. Heading over in 30. Traffic might be rough."

His response came immediately: "No rush. She's not going anywhere. Come around back—easier for loading her up."

Brenna spent the next twenty minutes in her truck, returning messages and calls. By the time she pulled onto Ninth Street, she'd added fourteen new volunteers to her roster. Fourteen more people willing to show up for something beyond themselves.

The parking lot behind Ocean City Animal Hospital was nearly empty. Brenna parked near the back entrance and took a moment to check her reflection in the rearview mirror.

She still wore the orange safety vest. Her hair was wind-blown from the marsh, and there was a smudge of something on her cheek that might have been mud or might have been leftover makeup from the news segment. She wiped at it with her sleeve, which only made it worse.

"Perfect," she muttered. "Very professional."

The back door opened before she could knock. Josh stood there in his usual scrubs, a smile breaking across his face when he saw her.

"There's our TV star."

"Please don't."

"Too late. My receptionist saw it and won't stop talking about it." He stepped aside to let her in. "Come on, your turtle's been asking about you."

The recovery room was small but well organized, with several cages and tanks arranged along the walls. Most were empty, but one contained a rabbit recovering from surgery, and another held what looked like an elderly cat sleeping on a heated pad. The room smelled faintly of disinfectant and something herbal, maybe the cleaning solution.

Martha's tank sat on a counter near the window, and Brenna moved toward it immediately. The terrapin was awake, her dark-spotted gray head visible above the shallow water. The epoxy repair on her shell had held perfectly, the fractures stabilized and clean. No swelling, no sign of infection. She looked alert, strong.

"She's been eating well," Josh said, coming to stand beside Brenna. Close enough that she caught the scent of clean cotton and aftershave. "Swimming normally. She's ready."

"You really did incredible work with her."

"She's a good patient. Never tried to bite me once, which is more than I can say for most of my reptile cases." He leaned against the counter, his shoulder nearly touching hers. "I've been reading more about terrapins since she came in. Fascinating species."

"You've been doing research on your own time?"

"What can I say? She caught my attention." He shrugged, but his eyes held hers a beat too long.

"Well, I wasn't sure anyone would take her on."

Brenna reached into the tank and gently lifted Martha out. The terrapin's legs paddled once, twice, then stilled.

"Hey, girl," Brenna said softly. "Ready to get out of here?"

"I set up a transport container for you." Josh gestured to a plastic bin on the counter, lined with damp towels. "Keep her in there during the drive, then transfer her to your recovery tank at the research center. She'll need another four to six weeks before release, but the hard part's over."

"I can't thank you enough for this."

"No thanks needed." He crossed his arms, watching her. "Rachel said you explained everything really clearly on the news. Made her want to go out and save turtles herself."

"Tell her to sign up. We can always use more volunteers."

"Not sure I can spare her." His eyes crinkled with amusement. "But I'll pass along the message."

Brenna lowered Martha into the transport container. The shell felt solid under her palms, the repairs holding strong. Days ago, this terrapin had been dying on the side of Bay Avenue. Now she was going to make it.

"I should get going," Brenna said, though she made no move toward the door.

"Right." Josh straightened, running a hand through his hair in a gesture that seemed almost nervous. "I'll walk you out." He picked up the transport container with Martha inside.

The hallway to the back entrance felt longer than it had on the way in. Brenna was acutely aware of Josh beside her, of the way their footsteps fell into an easy rhythm.

Outside, the late-morning sun had burned through the

earlier haze. The parking lot was still quiet, just Brenna's truck and Josh's pickup parked side by side.

"I can take her from here," Brenna said.

"I know." Josh reached past her to open the truck's passenger door and set the container on the seat. "She's lucky you found her."

"She's lucky you knew how to fix her."

"Team effort, then."

They stood there, neither quite ready to end the conversation. A seagull called overhead. Somewhere in the distance, a car honked.

"Listen," Josh said finally. "I don't want to come off as unprofessional, and I don't even know if you're seeing someone—" His eyes flicked briefly to her left hand then back to her face. "But if you ever wanted to grab coffee sometime, talk about something that isn't turtles..." He trailed off, a faint flush creeping up his neck. "I'd like that."

Brenna looked away then back. "I'd like that too."

"Yeah?"

"Yeah."

Josh's smile widened. "Okay. Good. I've still got your number from before. I'll call you. When you're not too busy saving species."

"I'll make time."

She climbed into the truck, Martha's container secure on the passenger seat. As she backed out, she glanced in the rearview mirror. Josh was still standing there, hands in his pockets, watching her go.

The drive to the research center took fifteen minutes. Brenna spent most of it thinking about coffee, about the way Josh had looked at her.

By the time she got Martha settled into the recovery tank at the center, she'd received twenty-three more volunteer inquiries. The news segment was still being shared on Facebook, the comment section filling with people tagging their friends, offering to help, asking where they could learn more.

She sat down at her desk and started responding to messages. Outside her window, the bay stretched silver-blue toward the horizon. Somewhere out there, in the marshes and tidal creeks, terrapins were going about their lives, unaware that people were finally paying attention.

It wasn't everything. It wouldn't solve the problem overnight. But it was something. And sometimes, something was enough.

* * *

Romano's looked different with afternoon light streaming through the newly cleaned windows. Lauren stood in the center of the main floor, her phone in one hand and a list in the other, surveying what they'd accomplished.

The shelves were organized now, each section clearly defined. The ribbon wall still dominated one side, every color and pattern imaginable arranged just as her grandmother had kept it all those years ago. Party supplies filled the back corner —Smurfs and Wuzzles sharing shelf space, relics of childhoods from another era. Vintage beach toys lined the center aisle, and the craft section with its wreaths and nautical decorations had been dusted and straightened. The price tags had been updated, the floors swept and mopped until they gleamed. The original cash register, a gorgeous brass-and-wood piece from the 1950s, sat polished on the counter near the entrance.

Claire had left an hour ago to pick up the kids from a beach day with Nancy and Joe. That gave Lauren time to handle the final piece of preparation: announcing the opening.

She opened Facebook on her phone and navigated to Chipper's business page. The restaurant had accumulated a decent following over the years, mostly locals and summer visitors who wanted updates on hours and specials. Now she'd use that audience to launch something new.

She typed carefully, wanting to get the wording right.

"Some of you may remember Romano's Party & Gift Shop, the store my grandparents ran next door to Chipper's back in the 80s and early 90s. Well, after sitting closed for nearly thirty years, we're opening it again. Romano's is back, starting tomorrow at 1 PM. Come see us Thursday through Sunday, 1-5 PM. We've got the original ribbon wall, classic beach toys, retro party supplies, kitchen collectibles, and plenty of Ocean City nostalgia. See you there!"

She attached a few photos she'd taken earlier: the ribbon section with its rainbow of options, the party supply aisle with its retro charm, a shot of the storefront from the street.

Her finger hovered over the post button. This was it. Once she announced it, the store became real. No more planning, no more maybe-someday. Just open doors and whatever happened next.

She pressed post.

The response started immediately. Likes and comments appeared within minutes, people sharing their memories of the original store, expressing excitement about the reopening, tagging friends who they knew would want to see this.

"I REMEMBER THIS PLACE! My mom used to buy all our birthday party supplies here!"

"Romano's is reopening?? I'm telling everyone I know!"

"The ribbon wall!! My mom used to spend hours there picking out colors for her craft projects!"

Lauren smiled at that last one, a warm rush of nostalgia washing over her.

She spent the next twenty minutes photographing some of the high-value pieces from the storage room. Most of the kitchen inventory was still in original packaging—retail boxes with price stickers intact, cartons that hadn't been opened in over thirty years. She and Claire had carefully unsealed a few to verify contents and condition, but the rest remained untouched, waiting for buyers who would appreciate what decades of storage had preserved.

She photographed one of the Lucky in Love Pyrex sets first, the pink hearts and green shamrocks striking against the white background. Then the Fire King jadeite in that distinctive green milk glass. Each photo required careful staging, good lighting, multiple angles. After the photos, she weighed each piece on the kitchen scale she'd brought from home, measuring dimensions for shipping calculations. She wrote detailed descriptions noting the unopened boxes, the pristine condition, the rarity of finding complete sets stored away since the eighties.

She posted them to eBay, pricing them according to Claire's research but leaving room for negotiation.

Within ten minutes, offers started coming in on the Lucky in Love pattern. $4,800. $5,100. Then $5,200.

That last one made her pause. She'd listed it at $5,800 based on comparable sales, expecting to negotiate. But $5,200 was already more than she made in two weeks at Chipper's. For a set of dishes that had been sitting untouched for decades, waiting.

She was still debating whether to accept or counter when her phone buzzed with a new notification. Someone had hit Buy It Now at full asking price.

$5,800. Just like that.

Lauren stared at the screen then laughed out loud in the empty store.

Through the windows, she could see people walking past on the sidewalk, their shadows lengthening in the late-afternoon light. A kid on a bike rode past, a boogie board strapped to his back. Two women jogged by in matching visors, deep in conversation.

This was Ocean City in May, that sweet spot between quiet off-season and the chaos of summer. The town was waking up, stretching, getting ready for the crowds that would arrive in a couple weeks. And Romano's would be part of it.

The bell above the front door chimed. Lauren looked up to see Matt walking in, carrying a brown paper bag and two bottles of honey green iced tea.

"Thought you might be hungry," he said, setting everything on the counter. "I got sushi from that place you like. The one near the bay."

"You're a saint."

"I prefer 'hero,' but I'll take it." He grinned, already unpacking the containers.

They stood at the counter, the sushi containers spread between them, the store quiet around them.

"This place looks incredible," Matt said, looking around as he unwrapped his chopsticks. "Totally different from what I saw last week."

"Claire and I basically lived here for the past few days. I'm pretty sure I've inhaled enough dust to qualify for some kind of medical condition."

"Worth it, though."

"Yeah." Lauren bit into a salmon roll, savoring it. "It really is."

Matt told her about practice. He'd been throwing in his backyard every morning now, building up arm strength, working on control. The wildness from that first game—the one inning they'd played before the sprinklers came on—was slowly improving.

"I actually hit my target three times in a row yesterday," he said, something like pride in his voice. "And again today. My mechanics are finally getting more consistent."

"That's great. How's the shoulder holding up?"

"Sore, but manageable. I've been icing it after every session, doing the stretches the physical therapist taught me back in the day." He shrugged. "It's not what it was. It'll never be what it was. But it's good enough for beer league."

"You sound okay with that."

"I am." He reached for another roll. "I've got Jungle Surf, I've got the team, I've got you. What's there to be angry about?"

Lauren playfully nudged his arm, feeling her cheeks warm. "Big day tomorrow. You nervous about the game?"

"A little." He pulled out his phone to double-check the schedule. "Game's at eight. Looks like I'm pitching the first few innings. No pressure."

"I'll be there cheering you on," Lauren said, smiling. "You'll be great."

"Or I'll hit someone with a pitch and get thrown out. Either way, it'll be entertaining."

They finished eating and cleaned up, tossing the containers in the trash bag Lauren had been filling all day. The sun was getting lower now, the light shifting from gold to something deeper, more orange.

"Want to take a walk?" Lauren asked. "Maddie finished the mural. I haven't had a chance to see it yet."

"Sounds good," Matt said.

They locked up the store and headed toward the boardwalk. The evening crowd was starting to gather, couples walking hand in hand, kids darting between benches while their parents called after them.

The mural was visible from a block away.

Lauren had seen it in progress, had watched it grow over the weeks of Maddie's work. But the finished piece was something else entirely. The colors were richer than she'd expected, deep blues and greens layered so carefully they seemed to hold their own light. The wave towered over the boardwalk, massive and alive, spray rendered in whites and silvers that caught the fading sun. It dominated the wall completely, transforming what had been a forgettable stretch of concrete into something people would remember.

"Wow," Matt said softly.

People had gathered to take photos. A little girl tugged at her father's hand, pointing at the wave's crest. An older couple stood arm in arm, their heads tilted back to take it all in.

"She did it," Lauren said. "After everything, she actually finished it."

"More than finished. This is going to be one of those landmarks people talk about for years. 'Meet me by the wave mural.' 'Did you see the painting by the arcade?'"

"It's part of the boardwalk now," Lauren said.

CHAPTER TWELVE

Lauren adjusted the scrunchie holding her side ponytail and stared out the front window of Romano's. The line stretched around the corner, at least thirty people waiting on the sidewalk, some talking with each other, others peering through the glass to catch a glimpse of what was inside. A man in a Phillies cap held a folded newspaper under his arm. Two women who looked to be in their sixties stood near the front, chatting animatedly and pointing at the rainbow of ribbons visible through the window.

"You're seeing this, right?" Claire said, coming up beside her. She'd gone full eighties with her outfit: a neon-pink cropped sweatshirt over a lime-green tank top, her own side ponytail secured with a scrunchie that matched Lauren's. Her vintage jean shorts, acid-washed and high waisted, had been found at a thrift store, just right for the occasion.

"I'm seeing it," Lauren said. "I just don't believe it."

The speakers crackled to life, and the opening synth notes of "Take On Me" filled the store. Lauren had spent two hours the night before curating the perfect mix of eighties and nineties hits. Evan stood near the old cash register, adjusting the volume on the portable speaker system they'd rigged up.

"Too loud?" he asked.

"It's perfect," Lauren said.

The banner above the door was impossible to miss. Claire had thrown the design together in an hour, channeling every cheesy mall storefront she could remember from 1987, and they'd had it printed as a vinyl banner at FedEx Office. "ROMANO'S" blazed in hot pink and electric blue, with "GRAND RE-OPENING" splashed beneath in yellow. It was peak eighties—exactly right for what they were selling.

"One minute to opening," Claire said, glancing at her watch. "You ready?"

Lauren took a breath. The store looked incredible. Every shelf was in place, every price tag where it should be. The greeting card spinners stood ready near the entrance, stocked with designs that hadn't been printed in decades. Gift wrap in geometric patterns lined one wall, rolls of shiny paper in teals and magentas that screamed 1986. The sticker display case near the register was already drawing glances from kids in line outside, its scratch-and-sniff sheets and puffy letter stickers visible through the glass. All of it waiting.

"Ready," Lauren said.

She walked to the front door and flipped the lock. The first customers pushed inside before she'd even stepped back, the two older women leading the charge.

"Oh my goodness," one of them breathed, stopping just inside the doorway. "It's exactly like I remember. Marie, look at this."

Her friend was already moving toward the ribbon wall, hands clasped in front of her chest. "The ribbon section. It's still here. I used to come here with my mother every Christmas to buy ribbon for our wreaths."

The store filled quickly. People spread out through the aisles, calling out to each other over discoveries, pulling out phones to take pictures. A family with three kids gravitated toward the vintage toys, the parents showing them items they'd owned as children. A man in his forties stood frozen in front of the party supplies, holding a pack of Teenage Mutant Ninja Turtles napkins like it was a religious artifact.

"Is this the original inventory?" someone asked.

"All of it," Lauren said. "A lot of it's been here since the eighties."

"Unbelievable."

Lauren spotted a few familiar faces in the crowd—regulars from Chipper's who must have seen her Facebook post. Mr. and Mrs. Hennessy, who came in every Saturday for blueberry pancakes, were browsing the nautical section. Frank, who always ordered the same egg white omelet, was flipping through a rack of eighties greeting cards.

Joe had stationed himself near the party supply section, wearing a polo shirt and khakis, his reading glasses pushed up on his forehead. He'd been hesitant when Lauren first asked him to help, insisting he didn't know anything about retail anymore, but the moment customers started flowing in, something shifted in his expression. He moved through the crowd naturally, stopping to chat with people, pointing out items they might have missed, sharing stories about the original store. Lauren saw him help an elderly man locate a set of brass fishing lures from the tackle display, the two of them reminiscing about some shared memory from decades past.

Near the front counter, Claire was helping a young mother sort through a bin of old school supplies—holographic pencils, scented erasers shaped like Garfield and Snoopy, fuzzy pencil toppers in bright colors.

"I used to collect these exact erasers," the woman said, holding up a pink strawberry-scented one. "My daughter is going to lose her mind."

Claire helped her gather a handful into a small basket, then made her way back to the register, where a line had formed. The tablet beeped as she rang up another sale. "Lauren, can you bag this?"

Lauren slid into position, tucking tissue paper around a set of Care Bears plates before placing them in a paper bag. The motion was familiar, almost automatic. Ring up, bag, hand off. Ring up, bag, hand off. How many times had she watched her grandmother do exactly this?

Bridget had planted herself near the craft section, offering to help customers carry items and answering questions with the enthusiasm only a twelve-year-old could muster. She'd insisted on dressing for the occasion too, wearing a neon-orange head-band and an oversized T-shirt she'd found at a thrift store the week before.

"Do you have any more of those miniature lighthouse figurines?" a customer asked her.

"Let me check in the back," Bridget said, heading for the storage room.

"We saved the best job for Mom," Lauren said, nodding toward a small table they'd set up in the corner, near the ribbon wall. Nancy sat at the workstation, complete with wire, ribbon samples, and all the supplies needed for bow-making. They'd unearthed most of it from the storeroom, the same tools Beverly had used all those years ago.

Nancy's movements were sure and practiced, muscle memory returning after decades of disuse. Loop, twist, secure. Loop, twist, secure. A bow took shape in her hands, full and symmetrical, the kind you'd see in a department store window.

"I haven't made bows in forty years," Nancy had said when she'd first sat down that morning. "Not since I used to help Beverly on the busy weekends." But within minutes her hands had found their groove, and now she had a small crowd gathered around her, customers waiting to see their custom orders take shape.

The afternoon flew past in a blur of customers and conversations. A woman bought a Pound Puppy still in its original packaging, explaining that she'd lost hers in a house fire years ago and had never found a replacement. Evan kept the music going, transitioning seamlessly from "Walking on Sunshine" to "Girls Just Want to Have Fun" to "Sweet Child O' Mine."

By four thirty, the crowd had thinned and they were getting ready to close up. Lauren took a rare moment to step back and survey the scene.

The store looked lived-in now, a pleasant dishevelment that came from people actually shopping rather than just browsing. Shelves had gaps where popular items had sold. The floor showed footprints from dozens of visitors. The energy in the room felt different than it had at opening, calmer but still charged with something like satisfaction.

Claire joined her, pushing a loose strand of hair out of her face. "We sold out of the E.T. party supplies."

"All of them?"

"Every last plate, napkin, and cup. Good thing there's more in the boxes behind the shelves." She nudged Lauren with her elbow. "I stopped counting after the first hour, but I think we've done over two thousand dollars in sales."

Lauren felt her knees go slightly weak. "In one afternoon?"

"In one afternoon." Claire grinned. "Not bad for a store full of stuff nobody wanted for thirty years."

Lauren looked around at her family scattered through the store—her father chatting with a few lingering customers, her mother tidying up her bow-making station, Claire leaning against the counter, Bridget and Evan straightening shelves. They'd done it. They'd actually done it.

* * *

Under the lights, the field had a magic to it.

Lauren had seen plenty of baseball games in her life, but there was something about a night game that felt special. The sky had deepened to a rich indigo, and the field lights cast everything in a bright, almost theatrical glow. The grass seemed greener, the baselines crisper, the whole scene possessing a sharpness that daytime games never quite achieved.

She found a spot in the bleachers behind home plate, spreading a blanket across the aluminum bench. Claire settled beside her, Bridget and Evan already making their way toward the concession stand. Nancy and Joe had claimed seats a few rows up, binoculars in hand despite the close proximity to the field.

"Binoculars at a baseball game?" Lauren had teased when she saw them.

"I want to see Matt's grip on his pitches," Joe said. "For once, these aren't for the birds."

The crowd was larger than Lauren had expected. The bleachers were nearly full, with more people gathering along the fences down the first and third base lines. A group of teenagers had set up lawn chairs in the grass beyond the outfield. Families claimed spots near the dugouts, children running between groups while parents chatted and checked their phones.

"Word got out," Claire said, nodding toward a cluster of men near the entrance who were pointing at the field and talking animatedly. "Someone posted on the Ocean City Facebook group that a former Phillies pitcher was playing tonight."

"You're kidding."

"Nope. Check the comments. People are legitimately excited."

The concession stand was doing brisk business. Lauren could see Bridget and Evan in line, deliberating over their options. The stand was run by volunteers from the league, a rotating cast of wives, girlfriends, and team supporters who donated their time to keep the operation running. The menu was classic ballfield fare: hot dogs sweating under heat lamps, soft pretzels glistening with salt, french fries in red-and-white paper boats. The smell of mustard and popcorn drifted across the field, mixing with the salt air from the ocean just a few blocks away.

Somewhere above the lights, seagulls circled and called to each other, their cries cutting through the hum of conversation. The rhythmic wash of waves was audible in the quieter moments, a constant reminder that this wasn't just any baseball field. This was Ocean City, where even a beer league game felt touched by something larger.

"Hot pretzel?" Evan appeared with his arms full, distributing food to Claire and Lauren before heading up to deliver Joe and Nancy's order.

"Thanks, Ev."

The pretzel was soft and salty, the mustard sharp enough to make Lauren's eyes water. She ate it in careful bites as the players took the field for warmups. Matt was already on the mound, lobbing pitches to the catcher, loosening up.

He looked relaxed out there. Not the tense, rigid stance Lauren remembered from his early practices, when every throw seemed to carry the weight of his entire past. Tonight he moved fluidly, his shoulders loose, his release smooth. The shoulder injury was still there, of course, would always be there, but it no longer seemed to define every motion.

The umpire called for the game to start, and the first batter stepped up to the plate. Matt wound up and delivered, the ball popping into the catcher's mitt with a satisfying thwack. Strike one.

A cheer went up from the bleachers, surprisingly loud. She looked around and saw people she didn't recognize, their attention fixed on the mound, on the former professional pitcher who'd chosen to come back to the game in this small, improbable way.

Matt's first inning went smoothly. A groundout to short, a fly ball to center, a strikeout on a slider that still had enough bite to fool a batter who'd been swinging for the fences. The crowd applauded as he walked off the field, and Lauren caught him glancing toward the bleachers, his eyes finding hers.

She waved, and he smiled.

"He looks good," Claire said.

"He does."

The game settled into a comfortable pace. Shorebreak scored two runs in the bottom of the second, and the opposing team answered with one in the third. Matt pitched through the fourth inning before handing off to Austin, his work done for the night. He joined the dugout to cheers from his teammates, accepting handshakes and back-slaps with a quiet confidence that spoke to how far he'd come since that first chaotic debut.

Bridget had disappeared somewhere with a group of kids her age, probably exploring the edges of the field or raiding the concession stand again. Evan sat with Joe, the two of them deep in conversation about pitch types and defensive positioning. Nancy was making her way back from the concession stand with a fresh bag of popcorn, stopping every few feet to chat with someone she knew.

This was what she loved about living here. A community gathering around a simple pleasure, drawn together by nothing more complicated than a baseball game on a spring night.

Shorebreak won, 7-4. It wasn't a dramatic victory, no last-minute heroics or extra innings, just a steady accumulation of runs that had the other team playing catch-up all night. When the final out was recorded, the crowd cheered, and players from both teams lined up to shake hands.

Matt found Lauren after the game, still in his uniform, his hair damp with sweat. He looked tired but happy, the satisfied exhaustion that came from doing something you loved.

"Good game," she said.

"It was." He put an arm around her shoulders as they walked toward the parking lot.

The others were waiting near the cars, talking and laughing the way people do after a night like this. Joe had his arm around Nancy. Claire was listening to Bridget recount something that had happened during the game, nodding along with exaggerated interest.

Evan jogged up to join them, clutching a foul ball he'd apparently caught at some point that night. "Matt, will you sign this?"

"Sure, buddy."

They stood in the parking lot for another twenty minutes, nobody quite ready to leave, the warm night air settling over them. Someone had left the field lights on, and they cast long shadows across the gravel.

Lauren surveyed her family, such as it was now—her sister finding her footing, her parents discovering new passions, Matt rebuilding something he'd thought was lost forever. The store had been a success. The game had been won. A fine day all around.

They loaded into their cars and drove home through streets that were starting to fill with the first trickles of visitors. Rental houses had lights on in windows that had been dark all winter. The boardwalk businesses were extending their hours, testing the waters before the real crush began. Summer was close now, close enough to feel it in the breeze.

Tomorrow she'd open the store again. Tomorrow Matt would practice his pitches in the backyard, and Claire would take the kids to the beach, and Nancy and Joe would head out to the marshes, looking for that pink spoonbill. Life here moved in patterns like that—steady, familiar, always changing and somehow staying the same.

Ocean City had always been about that, really. The waves of this place just kept coming, one after another, reliable as the tides. And the people who lived here learned to move with them, to find their rhythm in the constant motion.

EPILOGUE

The afternoon rush had slowed to a trickle, leaving Lauren alone behind the counter at Romano's with a cup of iced tea and the day's sales pulled up on the tablet. The store had been open for two weeks now, and she was still getting used to the rhythm of it, how customers came in waves that seemed to follow some invisible tide schedule.

A woman in her late sixties wandered through the front door, the bell above it giving its familiar chime. She wore a sun-bleached cover-up over her swimsuit and carried a canvas tote bag printed with shells. Her silver hair was pulled back in a loose braid, and she had the look of someone who'd spent decades walking these shores.

"Take your time," Lauren called from behind the counter. "Let me know if you need help finding anything."

The woman nodded but didn't respond, already drifting toward the back corner where the seashells were displayed. They were Lauren's grandmother's original stock, sorted by type and size into wooden bins that still bore handwritten labels in faded ink. Scallops. Whelks. Clams. Sand dollars, carefully wrapped in tissue paper to protect their delicate edges.

Lauren watched as the woman picked up a conch shell, turning it over in her hands, running her thumb along its spiral curve. She returned it to the bin and moved to the next, then the next, her movements unhurried and deliberate.

"These are beautiful," the woman said finally, loud enough to carry across the store. "Original stock?"

"From the eighties, most of them. My grandmother collected them herself."

The woman looked up sharply. "You're Ida's grand-daughter?"

"You knew her?"

"Knew them both. Your grandfather used to save the good shells for me when I'd come in." A softness crept into her voice. "I was sorry when this place closed. It meant a lot to people."

Lauren smiled. "I'm trying to do right by it."

The woman made a small sound of appreciation. She lingered over a bin of moon snails, their polished surfaces catching what light came through the front windows. After a few more minutes, she gathered a handful of shells and brought them up front.

She set them down gently, then glanced toward the door, as if checking to see if anyone else was listening.

"You might want to start keeping your eyes open," she said, her voice dropping. "For sea glass, I mean."

Lauren looked up from the tablet. "Sea glass?"

"Mmhmm." The woman picked up one of the jingle shells she'd brought over, translucent and orange, and held it to the light. "I've been beachcombing this island for forty years. Got a friend who works with the weather service, keeps track of storm patterns, that sort of thing." She put the shell aside. "Ocean City's never been known for sea glass. Not like Bay Head. But those nor'easters we had this winter?" She shook her head slowly. "Word is they churned up things that haven't moved in decades. Told me to watch the beaches this summer. Said this year might be different."

Lauren nodded politely. Sea glass was pretty enough, she supposed. She'd found pieces here and there over the years, the way everyone did. Bits of green from old bottles, the occasional blue shard worn smooth by the surf.

"I'll keep that in mind," she said.

The woman studied her for a moment, something unreadable in her expression. Then she smiled, the kind of smile that suggested she knew something Lauren didn't.

"You do that." She nodded at the shells on the counter. "I'll take these."

Lauren rang her up and watched as the woman tucked her purchases into the canvas tote. The bell chimed again as she left, and Lauren was alone once more.

She finished closing out the sales for the day and wiped down the counter, her mind already moving to the evening ahead. But something about the exchange lingered. The way the woman had looked over her shoulder. The way she'd lowered her voice, like she was sharing a secret she wasn't sure Lauren deserved to know.

* * *

Pick up book 6 in the Ocean City Tides Series**, Ocean City Sea Glass,** to follow Lauren, Matt, and the rest of the bunch.

Have you read the Cape May Series? If not, start with book 1, **The Cape May Garden**.

Coming soon! A **Sea Isle City** series.

ABOUT THE AUTHOR

Claudia Vance is a writer of Women's Fiction and Clean Romance. She writes feel good reads that take you to places you'd like visit with characters you'd want to get to know.

She lives with her boyfriend and 2 cats in a charming small town in New Jersey, not too far from the beautiful beach town of Cape May. She worked on television shows and film sets for many years. She's an avid gardener and nature lover.

www.ingramcontent.com/pod-product-compliance
Lightning Source LLC
Chambersburg PA
CBHW021730190726
48288CB00009B/2984